FINALLY. FINALLY. ALL THE THINGS I'VE DONE, ALL this blood and betrayal and wrong will be made right. We have a plan (don't think about the plan, never think about the plan). It will happen now.

It is happening.

Also by Kiersten White

~

MIND GAMES

PARANORMALCY

SUPERNATURALLY

ENDLESSLY

THE CHAOS OF STARS

ILLUSIONS OF FATE

PERFECT LIES

KIERSTEN WHITE

HARPER TEEN
An Imprint of HarperCollinsPublishers

HarperTeen is an imprint of HarperCollins Publishers.

Perfect Lies

 For information address HarperCollins Children's Books, a division of HarperCollins Publishers, 195 Broadway, New York, NY 10007.
www.epicreads.com

Library of Congress Cataloging-in-Publication Data
White, Kiersten.
Perfect lies / Kiersten White. — First edition.
pages cm. — (Mind games)
Summary: "Sisters Annie and Fia have had their abilities manipulated by the Keane Foundation for too long—and now they're ready to fight back against the twisted organization that has been using them as pawns"— Provided by publisher.
ISBN 978-0-06-213585-8 (pbk.)
[1. Psychic ability—Fiction. 2. Sisters—Fiction.] I. Title.
PZ7.W583764Per 2014 2013008056
[Fic]—dc23 CIP
AC

Typography by Torborg Davern
15 16 17 18 19 PC/RRDH 10 9 8 7 6 5 4 3 2 1

First paperback edition, 2015

For Noah

My past, present, and future

FIA

Every Day

ANNIE.

Annie.

Annie.

Annie.

I can't think about her, not ever. It isn't safe.

But when I'm asleep, no one can listen to my thoughts. I'm still afraid to sleep—too many ghosts peering creeping condemning. Sometimes though, the good times, I get Annie.

It's always the same.

Phillip Keane is gone, his webs destroyed, everything smoking and charred in beautiful ruins around me. We're safe. It's over.

But my hands are red, they're still so red I can't look at them, can't see them, can't breathe.

And then Annie is there. She's too young. I know she doesn't look like that anymore, but her face is open and innocent and clean. She wraps her hands around mine, so that I can't see the red anymore. We're *together*, and when we're together, all these things I've done, they don't matter anymore because they were worth it.

If I were Annie, I'd know whether this was a real future. All I know is it's the only one I want, the thing that keeps me going.

I will make that future happen.

ANNIE

Four Months Before

~

SHE DIDN'T KILL ME.

I was ready for the knife. I'd made my peace with whatever Fia needed to do to be okay. But . . . she didn't kill me. I try to keep my breathing shallow and hidden, try not to flex my fingers over the phone, though I want to.

Fia didn't kill me!

She must have come up with something else, some way out of this. I knew she would. I knew she would fix everything, I knew she would find a way to our future.

Two minutes ago I knew she was going to kill me.

After all this time, I can See and know everything, and still know nothing at all.

How long am I going to have to lie on the ground? Is she

coming back yet? My hip aches where it rests against the concrete, and people must be staring. I can hear them around me, footsteps, voices. Someone has to have noticed.

I hear the thud of hurried footfalls, then feel someone kneel next to me and let off a string of whispered profanity, soft and sad like a prayer.

A warm finger brushes against my neck fearfully, then puts firm pressure over my pulse. This time he swears loudly in surprise and . . . anger? He's mad that I'm not dead? "Are you okay?" he asks.

Hoping, trusting that this is part of Fia's plan, I move my lips as little as possible. "Shh," I whisper. "I'm dead."

There's a pause, and then arms go under my knees and behind my shoulders. I try to keep my body limp as I'm lifted into the air and cradled against a chest. I let my head and arms loll, still cradling the phone in the hand that's wedged between my body and his. I'm embarrassed about how hard I must be to hold, but I'm not breaking Fia's request until she tells me otherwise.

I need you to be dead.

I'll be dead, Fia.

"It's okay. My sister's epileptic. She'll be fine," I hear him say. I wonder who he is, where he's taking me with such a determined, slightly uneven limping stride.

He carries me for what feels like way too long, the warm sun playing on my skin cut through with an occasional breeze. Then I feel the whoosh of artificial air as we enter a building.

Without a word he lowers me to the floor. I rub my neck where it's cramping from hanging in a weird position.

"Where are we? When is Fia getting here? What's the plan?" I lean forward expectantly.

"You tell me," he snaps.

I flinch away from his tone. Fia's cell phone rings and I fumble, unsure what button to push. With a huff he takes the phone from my fingers, then shoves it back.

"Fia?" I'm trembling and out of sorts beyond anything I've ever experienced. I got up this morning expecting to die. Now I'm somewhere I don't know, with someone I don't know, and all I have is a phone.

"Who is this?" a soft, male voice asks. A voice I instantly recognize from one of my visions.

"Adam?"

"Yes?"

I put a hand to my mouth. Adam. I'm on the phone with Adam, the guy I personally arranged to have killed. The guy Fia spared. The guy who, according to my vision, is now in cahoots with the Lerner group. Fia delivered me to Lerner, the same group that drugged and kidnapped her. *After* shooting her in an alley.

Fia has perfect instincts, I remind myself. I shouldn't have an easier time believing that she'd kill me than I have believing that she knows what she's doing handing me over to these people.

"Umm, hey." How does one start a conversation with a guy she tried to have murdered? "This is Annie? Fia's sister?"

"Oh." There's a pause, and then he says, "Oh! It's Annie. Fia has Annie!"

A soft voice, a woman's, murmurs in the background on his end. "Where are you?" Adam asks, brimming with happy excitement, unlike my angry companion. "We'll come get you two!"

I lower the phone and talk in the general direction of the guy who carried me here. "Where are we? They want to come get us."

"Give me the phone."

I hold it out and feel it once again snatched from my fingers. His voice gets quieter as he walks away but retains its low intensity. I stand, trying not to feel awkward, wondering where we are. The doors open and someone walks past with a quiet "Excuse me."

I back up a few steps, hoping that I'm not in the middle of some hallway, and increasingly annoyed with Angry Guy for abandoning me here.

"Sorry, sir," a woman says over Angry Guy's continued hushed conversation. "You can't use your phone in the library. Please step outside."

"I'm done," he snaps.

I hunch my shoulders and shove my hands into my pockets, hoping they're not both looking at me. I wish I were wearing my sunglasses. Where are you, Fia? Hurry up so you can explain what's going on and what we're doing next.

"Here," he says right next to me, making me jump. "Here." The second time he says it a little softer and I finally clue in and hold out my hand. He gives the cell back, and I stick it in my pocket. Then . . . nothing. He says nothing.

"So. Umm." I wait for him to fill the silence.

"They're coming."

"Fia's meeting us here?"

"No. Fia is not meeting us here." His words have a strange quality, like they're being forced through clenched teeth.

"I'm sorry," I say, glaring because I'm not sorry, I'm frustrated. "I'm not up to speed on what's going on, and I'd really like to be clued in."

"I can't help you with that."

"But you're helping Fia."

"I am *not* helping Fia."

My heart thuds fearfully in my chest. "But . . . I thought . . . I mean, you were part of it. You picked me up." Oh, no. Oh, no. I gave him the phone. For all I know, he was delivering a threat or a ransom demand. All Fia did was give me the phone, which was meant to connect me with Adam. Not whoever this is. Tears brim in my eyes.

No. Think like Fia. What would Fia do?

Besides stab the guy.

"I'll scream," I say, standing straighter and facing him. "You shouldn't have brought me to a public place. Leave now or I'll scream." I pull the phone back out of my pocket and feel for bumps on the buttons, hoping the call feature will be prominent and that it saved Adam's number. "I won't be leverage, not for you or anyone else."

He swears, then grabs my fingers. I nearly shout until I realize he's pressing my index finger onto a button. I hear a number dialing.

"Crazy must run in your family," he says.

"You *do* know Fia!" I blurt, then bite my lip. He exhales in a silent laugh at my immediate association of crazy with my own sister.

"She stabbed me in the leg." Well, guess I was right about what Fia would do. "Then I shot her. Then I helped bring her in, against my better judgment, and let her see what we do. And *then* I followed her after she attacked me and ran. I got to watch as she murdered an innocent girl because I didn't stop her."

I hear Adam saying "Hello?" but don't put the phone up to my ear. This guy's anger makes no sense. If he's with Lerner, and that's where Fia wants me, why is he so mad?

"But she didn't. Murder me, I mean. I'm still alive." *Obviously.*

"Not for the minute it took between watching you fall and finding your pulse."

"Oh. I'm sorry." I mean it. I wasn't thinking about what it must have been like for him. "If it makes you feel any better, I thought I was dead, too."

"Why would that make me feel better?"

The sliding of glass doors precedes Adam's voice. "Cole! And you must be Annie?"

Hearing Adam in person is different from on the phone. I'm flooded with memories of the visions I've had of him—the one where I saw girl after girl with abilities being brought into the light and then disappearing into darkness, while Adam's name bounced around my skull, ricocheting painfully. And the other one, later, where I saw his face. I am meeting a guy whose name and voice I can put a face to. Other than James and his father, that has never happened to me.

It's too much, all of it. I don't know how to feel, what to think. I'm not with my sister, who I thought was going to kill me today. Instead, I'm with the guy I tried to have killed. The guy who spells disaster for hundreds of girls like me. The guy whose voice is kind and whose gentle face I will forever be able to see.

An arm comes around my shoulder and I jump.

"It's okay," a woman says. "You're safe."

"Where's Fia?" Adam asks.

"How do you all not know?" I ask. "I thought she had a plan. You are the plan. Right?"

"She didn't tell us anything," the woman says. "Do you have any idea what she'll do next?"

I shake my head. Fia's future is always a mystery to me.

FIA
Five Days Before

"MISS FIA, YOUR SHOULDER—" THE SECURITY GUARD says, eyes wide.

Ignoring him, I skip inside, the opulent, open lobby of the school swallowing me whole. James turns a corner, his suit all well-tailored lines of professionalism, sleek and slippery and mature. I hate it when he wears a suit. When he wears a suit he is Mr. Keane. His easy smile freezes before it can touch his eyes. He's scared for me.

It's adorable.

"What happened?" he asks. Ms. Robertson (I hate her I hate her I hate her I hate her) is behind him, a sheaf of papers clutched to her starched chest.

I shrug—it hurts—then flop onto one of the leather couches.

I'll get blood on it. I've poured a lot of blood into this school, but it's still thirsty, it's always thirsty.

"Ran into an old friend. And his knife. Why do so many of my old friends have knives?"

Ms. Robertson stomps toward me, glaring at my arm like it's personally offensive. "My office. We'll see if we can patch you up without stitches. Who did this?"

I smile at her. *Hello, Doris! Hello, Doris! Hello, Doris! Hello, Doris! Hello, Doris! Hello, Doris! Hello, Doris! Hello, Doris! Hello, Doris! Hello, Doris! Hello, Doris! Hello, Doris! Hello, Doris! Hello, Doris! Hello, Doris! Hello, Doris! Hello, Doris!*

She glares at James. "Make her stop."

James raises an eyebrow at me. "Fia?"

"What? All I said was hello. It's polite to say hello. Hello, Doris."

Huffing, she leaves and I stand, slightly woozy, to follow her. "Who was it?" James whispers.

"Dmitri. Russian mobster? He was mad that I stole millions of dollars from him. Silly man, doesn't he know money is imaginary?" It's paper that turns into numbers on screens. It's there, then it's gone. I put it places, I take it out, I move it somewhere else. Imaginary. Most things are imaginary, when you think about it.

Sometimes I think I'm imaginary.

"Dmitri," he growls, nodding. "If I had been there . . ."

"I still would have fought him and won, but then I would have had to worry about you, too."

James gives me a wry half smile. "At least let me pretend I can defend you sometimes."

I pat his cheek. "You're so cute when you're delusional."

"And you're sexy when you're on a post-fight high." His eyes search mine, more serious than his tone would indicate, and I know he's looking to see whether or not I'm falling apart. He doesn't need to.

I'm better than I was a month ago. A week ago, even. It was bad, but James held me together. He whispered dark, secret things to me and helped me escape myself with promises of flames and freedom. I narrow my eyes but smile, to let him know I know what he's looking for and that he won't find it.

"Don't tell Doris about Dmitri. I'll be there in a minute." James brushes a kiss along the top of my head. I lean into him, breathing in, wanting to lose myself there, needing to lose myself there. "Where were Johnson and Davis?" he asks.

I take a step back. "How am I supposed to know? It's not my fault if my shadows can't stay attached to me. Call Wendy Darling. Maybe she can sew them to the bottoms of my feet."

He swears, pulling out his phone. "They're there to protect you."

"Do I look like I need protection?" I hold out my hands, one with streaks of blood on it, and give him my best crazy crazy

crazy crazy grin. "You know, I like Dmitri. I crippled him, but I like him."

Whoever he's calling picks up and he starts yelling about doing a job and consequences and cleaning up messes. I wonder if the Russian guy is the mess or if I am. There's a smear of blood on James's suit jacket from where I hugged him, and I think it looks nice there, like it belongs.

I leave him and make my way to Ms. Robertson's office. She's already got a massive medical kit out on her desk and I sit, peeling off my shirt. It's hot in here, the heater in the corner working too hard, drying out the air and making everything feel small and scratchy.

"What did you do this time?" she asks through gritted teeth, fingers surprisingly gentle as she cleans the wound on my shoulder.

"Someone took my parking space."

"You don't have a car."

"That doesn't mean I should let someone take my parking space now, does it?"

She tears off strips of medical tape, lining them up to pull the edges of the cut closed. "Why don't you tell me who did this?"

Do you really want to get into my head? I think. *It's not a friendly place. You'll regret it.*

She sneers. "Are you going to kill me?"

I twist away from her, ripping open a package of gauze and

slapping it over my arm. "Is there a reason I should?"

"I don't know. Was there a reason you killed Eden?"

I tap tap tap tap against the table, then use my teeth to tear off enough tape to keep the gauze in place. I hated Eden. I hated her. I can't think about it, can't think about what happened, won't think about what happened. "She deserved it." I look at Ms. Robertson with the full force of my baby-blue eyes. "Do *you* deserve it?" *They'll let me,* I think at her. *They'll let me do whatever I want, and we both know it.*

"And your sister? She deserved it, too?"

I explode out of my chair, inches away from Ms. Robertson's face, which is no longer sneering. "She was in my way." Ms. Robertson is standing between me and the door, and I look pointedly at it. "You are in my way."

She moves.

As I walk past, her voice shakes with anger or fear (I can't tell, I'm not Eden, Eden Eden why'd she bring up Eden?) as she says, "And Clarice?"

I pause, my hand on the doorway. "I just didn't like her." Letting my mind go blank, not thinking anything at all, I turn and smile pleasantly at Ms. Robertson.

In the hall I nearly bump into a girl. She does a double take. "Fia? What happened? Where's your shirt?"

I glance down, my black bra in stark contrast to my pale torso, then laugh. "I knew I was forgetting something!" I try so hard not to remember their names, so very very hard, but I can't sleep because I see their faces. Mandy. Twelve. From New Orleans.

I wash myself clean of guilt, of pain, of fear, of emotion. I am the ocean. I am empty. I am nothing. Mandy lets out a little sigh of relief. She loves being around me. Silly Mandy.

"I cut my shoulder and there was blood on my shirt. I was going to find another one."

"You can borrow one of mine!" She holds out her hand, smiling shyly. I take it and let her lead me to her room, and I do not feel anything, not a thing, not a thing about this life or this girl or working in the school that I will burn to the ground.

When it gets to be too much, I picture the flames, imagine their heat. The noise they'll make as they devour everything Phillip Keane has built. It's better than the ocean for calming, and if any Readers look at me funny, I add marshmallows to my thoughts and am just a girl in want of a campfire.

I am a girl in want of complete destruction. But I am patient.

James finds me thirty minutes later, lying on my stomach on the floor of the main dorm common room, looking at fashion magazines with a gaggle of twelve- and thirteen-year-olds around me. They all jockey for position, each trying to slide in next to me, be close to me, be near me, because these girls know nothing.

They know nothing.

I think happy thoughts and feel happy things and I do not let myself near the swirling black edges of the hole that is my soul when I look at them.

I try not to spin. In third grade we did an experiment where we rubbed a needle on a magnet, then dropped it onto water. The surface tension let it rest on top of the water, and the magnet sent the needle spinning.

I used to be a compass, trained on the true north of protecting Annie. Without her I lost my north.

But James is my north now. The flames are my north now. Our dark secrets are my north now.

I tap tap tap tap on the magazine. Annie. Annie. Annie. Annie.

Don't think about Annie.

James holds out his hand to help me up and I take it, squeezing harder than I need to, willing it to be my anchor. This is what I chose, and I always choose right. James saved me. He'll always save me.

"Are you leaving already?" Mandy asks, a whine creeping into her voice. "You never stay!"

"That's my fault," James says, giving the girls his winningest lie of a smile. "I've got to take Fia to New York."

"New York?" I ask.

His smile goes deeper, sharper. "My father wants us working there. With him."

I don't know what to do with this sudden flood of

uncontrolled emotion. Finally. Finally. All the things I've done, all this blood and betrayal and wrong will be made right. We have a plan (don't think about the plan, never think about the plan). It will happen now.

It is happening.

James pulls me close, his arm around my waist holding me up. I am dizzy with anticipation. The beginning of the end.

"Will you come visit us?" Mandy asks. "You said the school will always be your home."

I try to smile, but my eyes dart around the room, tracing the contours of the walls, my finger tap tap tap tapping on my leg. Always.

"Take me away," I whisper to James, and he does.

ANNIE

Three and a Half Months Before

I PULL THE PHONE OUT OF MY POCKET, TAP IT ON THE table. The noise reminds me of Fia. Who hasn't called. It's been two weeks.

Two.

A throat clears. "Hey, Annie." Adam always announces himself when he enters the room. I appreciate it.

"Can I sit?"

I nod and feel the motel couch give under his weight. Without a word I hand the phone to him. He's been as anxious about getting word from Fia as I have; he's the one who tracked down a charger so the cell wouldn't die.

"No missed calls or texts," he says, stating the obvious.

"Who's ready for some lunch?" Sarah chirps, bringing with

her the scent of grease. My stomach turns uneasily. I hate myself as soon as I think it, but I really miss the Keane school chefs. I also miss my own cell phone, with raised buttons so I could use it without help. And my white cane that folded neatly into a purse. And my braille display for my laptop.

And . . . I miss knowing where I am. Being stuck in the school for so many years has turned me into an unwilling agoraphobe. I spent all that time either knowing the exact confines of my space or out with someone I trusted completely. Being untethered is kind of terrifying.

I miss Eden.

"Where to today?" I ask, needing distraction. We're all staying in a suite in some motel outside Denver. Our travel pattern deliberately makes no sense. Cole decides on the spot where we're going, and we never stay anywhere for long or plan more than a few hours in advance. Sarah says it's the best way to avoid anyone on the lookout for us, though she seems confident no Seer is going to have an eye out for me.

I'm dead, after all. So is Adam.

"Do you want me to cut your food for you?" Adam offers, and I shake my head. He's constantly trying to help me. I wondered at first if maybe he had a crush on me, but it doesn't feel like that.

Then again, how would I know? This is the most I've been around guys close to my age since I went to the school.

"I have good news," Sarah says. "I haven't seen anything. I

think we're safe to go to home base."

"Finally," Adam says, his voice desperate with relief. I bite my lip guiltily. He lost his parents, his schooling, his apparently brilliant future. And it's my fault. I put him on Keane's radar.

Cole surprises me by talking. Once again I didn't realize he was in the room. "Settles that, then. We'll go to the California house and make reintegration plans for our two corpses."

"Actually, we're headed to Georgia."

Cole's voice is suddenly cold. "Why Georgia? I don't see any reason to involve them further."

"We need help, Cole. We can't do this on our own."

"We've been doing fine."

"Did you even hear what Annie was telling us? He has women in the White House! This is so much bigger than we can fight, and if working with Rafael is what we need, then—"

"You don't know enough about him."

"I haven't seen anything that makes me worried."

"You don't see everything."

A door slams. Judging by Sarah's sigh, I assume Cole is gone. "What was that about?" I ask.

Sarah sounds falsely bright. "Nothing. Cole likes being independent. Lerner has always been a really loosely connected network, to keep us safer. But we're starting to organize and get funding, and it makes him nervous. I'll go pack your things and we'll head out!"

"I'm already packed," Adam says. Sarah leaves, but he stays

on the couch next to me. "So much research data all around me, and I can't do a thing to study it. I need to work before I go crazy."

"You can't!" I blush, embarrassed at my outburst. "I mean, you can't keep pursuing it, right? That's how they found you." *I'm* how they found him, but the vision still swirls in my head, unsettling me.

He sounds thoughtful. "Sarah thinks we can manage it. And she feels like it's really important, like it might finally give us an advantage against Keane."

My thoughts are scattered, my nerves frayed. What if it did? What if that's what my vision meant? That we'd find the women and then help them disappear? Maybe I'm interpreting it wrong. It wouldn't be the first vision I was wrong about.

Probably won't be the last, either.

The car slams to a stop, my seat belt digging into my collarbone. "What is he doing here?" Cole snaps.

"Who?" Sarah asks. "Oh. I didn't know he was coming."

The car eases forward and then stops again. I hear doors open, so I unbuckle my seat belt and climb out, kicking my foot to find the curb.

"Cole," a man calls from nearby. He sounds older than Cole and Adam. "We've been waiting for you."

"Nathan," Cole says, his voice icy. "Why are you here?"

"Permanent security detail with the boss."

"Right." Cole's voice is edged with tension and anger. He must have a headache all the time if he carries as much tension in his neck as he does in his voice. "The *boss.* Great."

Sarah takes my arm. "Don't worry," she whispers in my ear. "Cole's just PMSing."

I snort, instantly more at ease. I don't think Cole will stick around any longer than he has to, which is a bit of a relief. He stresses me out.

"Come on in," Nathan says as we walk up three steps. "And who is this?"

I don't like the shift in tone of Nathan's voice that indicates he's talking about me. It's as though he's no longer addressing an equal but a child or a plaything.

"None of your business," Cole snaps.

I frown in his direction. I don't need him defending me, but I'm surprised that he'd sound so . . . protective on my behalf.

We walk past Nathan, who wears a spicy aftershave that clears out my sinuses. I instantly decide I don't trust men who wear too much cologne. What is he covering up?

The air shifts as we enter the house, less heavy with humidity and cooler. "Rafael!" Sarah says, sounding happy.

"Sarah! So good to see you again. And this must be Adam, which makes you Annie." The speaker has a soft, musical accent that makes it harder for me to get much from his tone. It also makes me wish I could see his face, because his voice is very, very hot. A cheek brushes mine and I start, surprised, as he kisses the air next to my face.

He backs away, laughing. "I hate shaking hands. Don't look so frightened, Adam, I promise not to kiss you. Where are you from, Annie?"

I smile nervously. "Colorado, originally. Lately of Chicago. I'm dead, though. Just for the record."

"Naturally." Rafael sounds amused, and I want him to like me so I can hear him talk more. "So you're Fia's sister."

The way he states it gives me pause. "Do you know her?"

He laughs again, a laugh that holds secrets. "We've met, yes."

"Did she stab you, too?"

This time the laugh is easy and loud. "No, nothing so dramatic."

"Good. She has a habit of doing that apparently."

"She destroyed my knee," Nathan grumbles from behind us. I'm not sure if I should apologize. I didn't to Cole for his stab wound, so I opt not to.

"Any word from our charmingly violent Fia?" Rafael asks.

Sarah answers. "We have a phone she gave Annie, but there hasn't been any contact."

"Hmm. Here, sit, I'll have Nathan get coffee." Rafael takes my arm and guides me to a leather couch in a carpeted room. "You know your sister better than anyone. Do you have an idea what she might be planning?"

I shake my head, then lean back against the couch. For what feels like the millionth time I rack my brains, trying to think of anything Fia said or did, any indication she might have given me about what her plan was.

I want to be with her, to hear her. I don't want my last memories of her to be the vision where I thought she killed me, or our tear-filled exchange under the arch.

And then I *see* her. It rushes in, slamming into my eyes. Fia, wearing a tank top and long, loose, patterned pants. Pajamas. The room is nearly dark, with a pool of warm yellow light drifting out from a single lamp. Fia walks toward it, then pauses, looks down.

At James. I've seen him before, and he hasn't changed, though in sleep he looks far more peaceful than I could have imagined. He's sprawled on the couch, glasses askew on his face.

She's going to kill him, I think. I don't want to see, don't want to watch her do this, but I can't avoid what the vision wants to show me.

She reaches down and gently pulls the glasses off his face, closing them and setting them on the floor. Then she leans over, brushes her lips against his forehead, and turns off the lamp.

With the sweetest, most content smile on her face I could ever have imagined.

Darkness reclaims my eyes, and for once I am grateful to be

back where I belong, back where life makes sense. She smiled. Not the dead-girl, hollow smile I'd seen in visions past. She looked . . . whole. With *him*.

"Are you okay?" Cole asks.

"I saw her," I whisper.

"Who?" I can feel Rafael leaning in close to me.

"Fia. She was with James." I cover my face, sick to my stomach. Because now I finally realize, I finally get it.

Fia saved me. She set me free.

But she also abandoned me.

"Fia's not coming."

FIA

Four Days Before

I WAKE UP JUST BEFORE DAWN, AND I CAN'T—I can't—I can't—I can't do this, I can't feel this, I can't be me right now. Clarice's face, her ruined face, then blood on my sister's hand. I thought I'd have the good dream tonight. Not this.

I stumble down the hall, into James's room. Crawl into his bed. He wakes up with a start. He is not like me: his first instinct is not to fight but to pull me close. He holds me until I can breathe again.

"It's okay." His voice is soft and sweet with sleep as he strokes my hair. "It's okay." His arms keep me from shaking apart. Sleep is okay when James is anchoring me, and here, now, there are no lies between us.

Whatever else he is, James is my one safe place in the world.

* * *

"Where did you go last night?" James asks, leaning against the wall as I finish flinging clothes into my suitcase.

"Hmm?"

"You sneaked out last night. I woke up at four and you were gone again."

"Didn't I tell you? I'm having an affair. With an accountant. He reads tax code aloud by candlelight; it drives me wild."

"Fia."

I shrug, shoving my clothes down so I can get the suitcase shut. I wonder if I should be sad to leave this city, if I'll ever come back. I don't care about taking anything with me. Nothing here is mine.

I remember the quilt on my bed when I was little. It was blue with white clouds, worn threadbare, warm but light enough to burrow under without feeling like I was suffocating. I remember the knotted rug by my parents' bed, beneath a battered wood chest my mom kept our memory boxes in. (My mom, my mom, I don't even remember what she sounded like anymore. She is a picture, a home movie clip, a ghost of a person in my memories that are so small they wouldn't even fill the box anymore.)

"Are you going to answer me?"

I look up, startled that James is still here. No, I will not miss this city. A place is a place is a place. I don't care. James and I together, that's what matters. We're on our way to destroy his father, dismantle Keane Enterprises, and then be free. I am sharp and ready. "You're the one who told me it's good to keep secrets."

"Not from me."

I grin, pointing a finger at him. "Especially from you."

He sighs and rubs his forehead. "Anything illegal?"

"Me? Never." I woke up and his arms weren't around me anymore and he was asleep and so far away, and the emptiness was too big, too scary, the waiting too much, so I went running.

He walks into the room and sits on the couch, pulling me into his lap. "Just how many secrets are you keeping from me?"

"I'd tell you, but it's a secret." I lean my forehead against his, letting myself feel quiet, looking for the thing inside me that tells me what we're doing is right. It's been so hard to find since I gave up Annie. "This is what we've been waiting for. This is what everything has been for."

"Of course. This is the biggest vote of confidence my dad has ever given me. We're finally sliding into place." His eyes get distant, and something nervous twists in the pit of my stomach.

"You're having second thoughts."

He shakes his head, focuses on me. "No. You and me, that's the way it has to be. We do what we're supposed to and no one will see what's coming until it's too late."

I scratch a finger under his jaw, my nail catching on his stubble. "Not even us."

"Not even us."

"What do you mean, I can't go in to see Mr. Keane?" I sing the Beatles' "Yellow Submarine" in my head over and over again, because I can't think about what I need to think about, which is not a what but a who. The girl behind the desk glares at me.

"He wants you to get a feel for the receptionist. She's too good for the Feelers or other Readers to figure out," James had said, looking past me as we rode the elevator up up up up to where he would disappear past locked doors to his father, leaving me behind.

Babysitting.

I'm *babysitting* a freaking Reader.

She pops her gum, bored. "You aren't cleared to go back to the offices."

Hey, I think. *On a scale of one to ten, how fond are you of an intact spinal cord?*

Her eyes widen and I laugh. "Just kidding. Probably you should stay out of my head. It's not a friendly place."

"Clearly." She has short hair, bleached white, with choppy bangs hanging over her kohl-rimmed eyes. From the looks of her she's maybe sixteen, pixie features and tiny frame; her feet hang a few inches above the floor. She's wearing metal almost everywhere metal can go—ears, nose, fingers, wrists, even studs on her black heels. It doesn't compensate for how small she is. Fragile. Fingers like twigs, equally snappable.

"Aren't you a little young to be Keane's personal assistant?" I ask, leaning against the rosewood desk she's slouching at.

She doesn't break eye contact. "Aren't you a little psychotic to be Keane's employee?"

I like her. The pixie is going to be my friend. I know it like I know I'm not going to see Mr. Keane today. I will be her friend, while plotting to either betray her if she's untrustworthy for the company, or be betrayed by her if I slip up and she sees thoughts she shouldn't.

Best friends.

"When is James getting out of his meeting?"

"Quit thinking of me as a pixie. It pisses me off."

Magic magic pixie dust! Tinker Bell! Tiny pixies with sharp teeth, stealing children and horses! I start humming the Pixies' "Where Is My Mind?" under my breath.

"You really are as obnoxious as everyone thinks you are." She sighs heavily, slides off her chair, and walks around the desk. Even in four-inch heels she barely comes up to my chin. "Let's go get dinner."

I let my eyes travel down the hall behind her. Mr. Keane is there somewhere. Mr. Keane who—nope not gonna think about it, not gonna think about anything at all. I can be patient.

Pixies. Pixie haircuts. Pixie sticks. Drumsticks. Music. Dancing. I want to go dancing! Ache for it.

"You know what?" she says. "I changed my mind. Go ahead and snap my neck. It's gotta be better than listening to you free-associate to try and scramble me."

I laugh and wrap my arm through hers, steering her past the security guard and toward the gleaming elevators. "Your mistake is in assuming my brain doesn't work like this all the time."

We ride down the elevator in relative silence, except when Pixie asks me to please think the lyrics to a song she wouldn't mind having stuck in her head. I settle on Queen in my head and pizza for dinner.

"So," I say around a thin and drooping slice. "Turns out I do miss something about Chicago. What the crap is this crust?"

"Don't ask me. I'm a vegan."

I reach out and tug the collar of her leather jacket. "And this cow died of natural causes?"

She shrugs defensively. "My grandma gave it to me for my thirteenth birthday. It was hers. The cows would have been dead of old age by now, anyway. Besides, eggs are disgusting, and have you ever actually thought about what dairy is? You are eating the product of liquid squirted from the *nipples of a cow*."

"Mmmm . . ." I stick my tongue out to catch a stray strand of goopy cheese. Pixie rolls her eyes, and I free-associate cow nipples in my thoughts to entertain her and keep my brain safe as I sit back and look out the window at the busy sidewalk. It's dark and bitterly cold, but that doesn't seem to matter to anyone out there. New York is more claustrophobic than Chicago, the buildings tall and looming so that you can't see anything beyond your street. This afternoon as I prowled the city, waiting for James to text me that it was time to go in, I passed the Empire State Building without even noticing until I almost knocked down a tourist.

How come Pixie is here? Why isn't she in the school?

"My name isn't Pixie. And it's because I'm too good for the school, you idiot. When they interviewed me for a scholarship, I started asking them about the Keane Foundation and what on earth Feelers were and assured them that I was more than qualified for whatever they had in mind. Then they put me up against their best Readers—"

"Did you get Doris?"

"Yes! Kill me now, her thoughts were like being trapped in an airless room with nothing but smooth jazz."

I cackle. "So, what, they gave you independent study?"

"Pretty much. Said I could cut my teeth at the front desk of Keane's main office, since I was too young to place somewhere big."

"And your family . . ."

Her eyes get tight and she snaps her head to look outside.

Not in a tragic, I've-been-ripped-away-from-them way. I tap tap tap tap a finger on the counter. She *wants* to be here, I can tell. Hmm. I will tread carefully. Super careful.

Ha ha ha ha, as if.

She clears her throat. "I lived with my grandma until she died when I was thirteen. Then I got saddled with my dad who'd sooner raise hunting dogs than a teenage daughter. So." She claps her hands together, smile too wide and eyes too bright. "I get to come to the great big city and do great big things, and he gets to take the sheets off the couch that doubled as my bed. Win-win!"

Am I supposed to hug her? Console her? (Annie would know what to do. *Would have.* Would have.) "Well, screw that. Let's go dancing."

She frowns as though trying to hear something better, then shakes her head and jumps off the stool. "That, I can do."

My phone buzzes and I pull it out. Text from James. *Stuck in meetings.*

Late dinner? I can eat twice if it means we can talk.

Eating with my father. Sorry. Will make it up to you tomorrow.

I narrow my eyes at the screen, tap tap tap tap on it. I need us to *move*, to *do*, to start this wheel spinning until it flies off its axis and destroys everything around us. I hold James's face in my thoughts, imagine his arms around me. Imagine his voice whispering "patience" in my ear before I elbow him in the stomach because I hate it when he tells me that.

I take a phone off the counter, where someone set it down to go get a refill.

"Did you just steal that guy's phone?" Pixie asks as we hunch our shoulders against the chill. She has her own phone out, looking for a nearby club.

One can never have enough phones, I think at her. She gives me a secret smile in return.

ANNIE
Three Months Before

~

I'VE BEEN VENTURING OUT MORE NOW THAT RAFAEL got me a white cane. Coming and going as I please is a luxury I intend to take advantage of. It's strange—for so long I hated seeing the future because it didn't belong to me. It belonged to Keane. Now I have my own future, and no idea what to do with it. Fia was always supposed to be with me. She's not.

I feel lost.

As I trail my fingers along the hall wall I hear voices. I pause—both are hushed but clearly angry. Taking a few steps forward, I lean near a doorframe and listen.

"—you know I'm right!" Cole.

"I don't! And you don't know, either. I'm tired of arguing with you." Sarah sounds exhausted.

"What about Annie? There's no reason for her to stay here. She can't accomplish anything. She sees even less than you do, and she's a huge target. She needs to be placed somewhere else."

I flinch at the tone of his voice. I didn't think Cole liked me, but I had no idea he wanted me gone that much. Rafael decided not to set me up somewhere else with a real life and a new identity. He wanted me close.

I was flattered, but lately I've realized I'm useless here. It makes me feel pathetic and small, but Cole's right. There's no reason for me to stay, other than to be protected.

I'm tired of needing other people to protect me.

"That's not our call," Sarah says.

"That's exactly what I'm talking about! Why isn't it our call? Why does he get to decide who stays and who goes?"

"You start bankrolling this operation and you can have more say," Sarah snaps. Something thuds to the ground, too small for a body, and then Cole swears.

"What is this?"

"Give it back."

"You're taking these?"

She sounds ashamed. "I haven't started yet."

"This is insane, Sarah."

"How am I supposed to help if I can't see enough? Rafael has a source on the inside that says Keane has all his Seers go on Adderall."

"He also has girls killed and thrown into the river. Is that our next step?"

"Aren't you the one who said we should do whatever we have to, whatever it takes to keep more girls out of his claws? Well, this is my *whatever it takes*."

Something small hits the other side of the wall I'm leaning against and I jump, turning and hurrying back to my room. The last thing I want is for Cole to catch me eavesdropping. I can only imagine what he'd say.

I flop onto my bed, tormented by futures both seen and unseen. They feel just out of my grasp, as usual.

"Fia," I whisper to the empty room, "what should I do?"

Then something changes. I'm still in the dark. It's not a vision, it can't be, I don't see anything. But I'm not on my bed anymore. It has to be a vision.

Someone reaches out and laces his fingers through mine and my world blossoms with color—inside the darkness. It's color and light and life that I feel inside me instead of seeing outside. I'm wild with giddy joy, a warm heat flaring like something long dormant in my heart has finally been switched on.

His fingers are not much longer than mine, his palm only a bit bigger, rough but warm, and the way our hands fit together . . .

Holy crap. I'm in love.

That's when I feel my bed underneath me again and realize I'm back in the present.

I had a vision where someone holds my hand and I know I'm in love with him. It's the single most romantic thing I have ever experienced.

And it wasn't even real.

But if I saw it—or felt it, really, because I've never had a vision where I was *me* like that, where I couldn't see—then it has to happen, right? I rub the palm of my right hand with my left thumb, torn between elation and nerves. Love. I can live with the promise of love. I just wish I knew when. And who.

And, with a sudden sharp ache, I wish more than anything I could tell Eden. It feels wrong to have something like this without her to whisper it to. For a moment I hate Fia for her choice. She not only took herself away from me, she made it impossible for me to ever see my best friend again.

Someone is going to hold my hand, and I'm going to be thrilled. And no one I love will know.

FIA

Three Days Before

~

"HOW DO YOU DO THAT?" PIXIE ASKS, FROWNING AT me over her drink. I got her a Shirley Temple. She didn't find it nearly as funny as I do. Last night she managed to scam some alcohol, but not tonight.

"Do what?" I eye the dance floor, annoyed she called me over. I am falling apart. I've barely even seen James since we got to New York. I need something, anything to distract me from the waiting. Visions of flames dance in my head, but I cannot light anything on fire yet.

Dancing is the only thing to take the edge off. (I could get in a fight. That's good, too. Pounding and moving and reacting, always reacting, no room for thought.)

"How do you stop thinking like that?" Pixie asks. "When

you're dancing, everything shuts down. I've noticed you doing it a few times, like you've switched to autopilot and there aren't any active thoughts in your brain."

"Isn't that the point of dancing?"

"Not for the guys you're with. You should hear their thoughts." She scowls, disgusted and miserable, shoulders slouched protectively inward as she stabs her straw through the ice.

I pat her head (four times, four is the magic number and I don't like it, four feels lonelier than three, no middle to huddle around, but I hate them both) and laugh. "They aren't people, they're just bodies. I don't care what they're thinking."

"I can't tell you how much I wish I could not care."

I sigh and sit down. "You have one minute to unburden your soul to me before I get too antsy and either hit you or go back to dancing."

"See, that's why I like you. You don't lie."

"I lie constantly. All the time. I'm nothing but one big mass of lies." I shouldn't tell her that. I should tell her that I'm good and obedient and do exactly what I'm told all the time. But I forget around Pixie, because she is lonely and small and fragile. I still don't know whether or not Keane can trust her, and whether or not that means I can't. She is such a silly, pointless assignment for me it's hard to take it seriously.

But I can't trust anyone. James and me. That's all there is, all there will be. Us against everyone. I need him. I tap tap tap tap against my leg. I *need* him to keep me away from the holes in my soul, but he's not here.

"You're honest about being a liar," Pixie says. "And you don't lie the way normal people do. You don't tell me my dress is cute and then think to yourself that I'm too flat to pull it off. I can't tell you how much I hate girls. I hate guys, too, because they tell you one thing but think another. There's always an agenda, and the agenda is always the same."

"Yup. They only care about your brains."

She laughs. "That's one of the things I like about working for Keane. They don't pretend to like me for anything other than my mad Reading skills."

I sit up straighter, narrow my eyes. "Have you actually met him? Mr. Keane?"

"Calm down, puppy. His name lights up your brain like Vegas. And the answer is no. Never been in the same room as him. Everything comes via phone or message. I get the feeling he doesn't want me crawling around in his head."

"Can't imagine why. You're a delightful tenant."

She flicks a piece of ice at me, then looks wistfully out over the crowd of writhing bodies. "I'd like to find a super hot guy with Asperger's whose thoughts are the same as his words."

"In that case we need to work on your targeting, because this audience? Probably not your best bet."

"What about you? What do you want in a guy? Besides a body to dance by."

James. I want James but he isn't here and the longer I go without him, the more scared I get. The fear sets in so quickly now, always lurking, waiting to swallow me. I hate being scared, hate it, it makes me sick and I want to cut it out of me with a knife, leave it bleeding and dripping on the table, a quivering mass of weakness. Every time I dream of Annie, I can't shake the scared. What if I chose wrong? What would that mean? A sudden image of gray eyes pops into my head. I wonder . . .

Dead dead dead dead. I snap my thoughts back into line. Dead. Adam's dead, Annie's dead, everyone's dead. I'm exactly where I'm supposed to be. I grin at Pixie. "Dance with me?"

Her dark eyebrows have disappeared under her blunt white bangs. "Sometimes you scare me."

"That's because you don't really know me yet." I hold out my hand to her. "When you really know me, I'll scare you *all* the time."

My phone vibrates in my pocket and I pull it out. James.

"What," I answer, annoyed. I don't want his voice on the phone, I want it in my ear.

"Has anyone ever told you how sexy you are when you dance?"

A hand comes around my waist and I grab the wrist, twist it, then turn to find myself right up against James, and everything is right again. I lean against him, tip my face toward him.

"Oh, hi," I say.

"Oh, ouch," he says.

I let go of his wrist. He laughs and puts his phone away. "I have a surprise for you."

I can hear the smile in his voice, the sly quality it gets when he's truly pleased with himself. I want to ask what it is, but audience, we have an audience.

I glance over at Pixie, who's watching us with her arms folded. She looks like a cat, all clever eyes and inscrutable expressions.

Cats are annoying.

"Guess our night is over, then," she says.

James smiles at her, but it is his cold smile. "You've been monopolizing my girlfriend's time."

I know in an instant that James doesn't like her, doesn't trust her. I'm torn between wanting to turn and leave with him and feeling oddly protective of my tiny, tired companion. I wonder what will happen if I decide Keane can't trust her. I don't want to think about it. "Go home," I say to her. "You look like crap."

She lets out a burst of bitter laughter, then looks up, scanning the crowd. "Do you know that guy?"

"Which guy?"

She shakes her head, eyes darting. "Can't tell. Someone here is thinking your name like crazy."

James looks wary, shoulders tensing protectively as his arms go tighter around my waist. He forgets that I can do more when he lets me go. Always at war, this need to have him close and push him away.

"Any of my shadows here?" I ask him, but even before he shakes his head I know that's not it. There's a whisper of caution running down the back of my neck, and I can't tell if I'm in danger or if I should pursue this. One of those horrible in-between feelings I'm getting more and more, that are neither right nor wrong, that make me feel off and disconnected like I'm experiencing my own feelings through a bad phone connection.

I tap tap tap tap. What to do.

"All right." I slip away from James and grab Pixie's arm. She squeaks in protest. "I don't feel like fighting tonight, and I really don't want to have to protect both of you. Cab. Straight home."

I drag her out, probably with more force than is strictly necessary but I'm unreasonably annoyed that I won't get to dance with James. His car, some sleek black money monster, is parked at the curb, but I hold my hand up for a cab.

"I'll be waiting," James says, lips brushing the back of my neck and making me shiver.

I want to go straight to him, but I can't. I like Pixie. I'm not going to let her get hurt tonight. Maybe she will get hurt later, maybe it will be my fault, but not tonight.

She rubs her arm where I grabbed her. "What do you do to the people you don't like?"

I flash my teeth like knives in the dark. "Do you really want to know?"

She kicks my shin in a halfhearted pout. "You think different around him, you know."

"Oh?" A cab pulls to the side and I open the door.

"Clearer. Happier. But scarier." She gets in the cab before I can ask what she means. At least she's safe. As far as I can tell.

James is waiting with my door open when I walk back to him. He has a scowl on his beautiful face, and I want to trace the line between his eyebrows with my finger.

"You need to finish up with her," he says, pulling away from the curb with a screech. I hate being in the passenger seat. I belong behind the wheel, sliding into spaces between cars, speeding through the dark.

I slump in my seat, put my feet up on the polished wood of the dash, hoping to scratch or scuff it, knowing James won't say anything if I do. I finally have him and he wants to talk about my waste-of-time assignment with Pixie? "I haven't been able to decide. Tell your father if he's so anxious for answers, he can ask me himself."

"She's too good. She could mess everything up for us, find out things we can't let anyone know."

"*I* barely know the things we know. She isn't pulling anything out of my head. There's nothing to pull! I'm still waiting!" I know it's irrational—it will take time. We are laying the groundwork for his father to be arrested, for the company to implode. It can't happen overnight.

But I just want it to be done. When it's done, I can get Annie back. We can all leave this behind forever.

"We have to be patient."

I want to rip out his hair. I want to grab the steering wheel and swerve into oncoming traffic.

I lean forward, clutching my knees to my chest, taking deep breaths. James puts his hand on the back of my neck, warm and steady, and the breathing gets easier.

"I know it's hard," he says, his voice so different when he's being gentle. I don't know whether I love it or hate it. It confuses me. Angry James I knew. Angry, distant James was easy to love because he was still safe. But this James that is mine feels dangerous.

I don't ever get to keep the things that are mine.

He squeezes my shoulder. "I promise you, it will all be worth it. The things you've done—they haven't been for nothing."

I look out the window into the night, not dark here but lit with thousands of glaring eyes, watching everything always. All these things I've done. So many things. Please, please, they have to be for something. I'll make them for something.

"How is your dad?" I ask, needing to get away from the horror movie of my life playing in my head.

"We're not talking about him tonight. Tonight is about us."

He pulls over and parks the car illegally, then gets out. I follow. We're at a building I don't recognize. It's closed, dark, locked up for the night. He's grinning, boyish in his anticipation.

"Well?"

"Do you remember the first time we met?"

I do. Every second of it.

I shrug.

"I broke into an all-girls school and we got drunk together." He pulls a bottle out of his jacket. I notice the copper plaque above the door, identifying it as St. Mary's School for Girls. I can't fight the smile that tugs on the edges of my mouth in response to his.

He closes the distance between us, leaning down, forehead against mine. "I was feeling nostalgic." I lean up and my lips meet his. I always lose myself in his lips, but it's the best way of being lost.

"So, what do you think?" he says, hand on the small of my back, pulling me closer. "Should we break into a school and get smashed?"

James is mine. He is my north, and as long as we are together, everything is okay.

ANNIE

Two and a Half Months Before

~

THE BLOOD IS POUNDING IN MY HEAD; I CAN FEEL IT building pressure behind my eyes. Still nothing. My arms and stomach muscles are trembling; I can't hold this handstand much longer, even with the help of the wall bracing me.

"*What* are you doing?"

I startle and fall down, my legs smacking against the wood floor of my bedroom. "Ouch."

"Are you okay?" Cole asks.

"This is my room," I snap from my undignified position on the floor.

"Door was open. Dinner's ready."

"Not eating."

"That'd explain the crankiness."

I flip him off, then stand. I don't have to put up with crap from someone who obviously hates me and wants me out of the house. Rafael and Adam and Sarah all like having me here. I'm determined to show that I have some value.

Unfortunately, this experiment proved fasting plus making all the blood rush to my head does not a vision trigger. Sucks. Guess I won't sleep tonight and add extreme fatigue.

"What are you trying to accomplish?" Cole asks.

"Are you still in here?" I grab a throw blanket off the edge of my bed and wrap it around my shoulders. Adam's way more thoughtful.

"Yes."

I sigh and flop down on the bed, light-headed. "Sometimes I can make myself see something if I push my body far enough."

"Doesn't sound healthy."

"I need to see . . ." Fia. I need to see Fia. But I also don't want to. I don't want to see her trailing after James like a well-trained pet. It makes me sick, makes me angrier than I've ever been, that she chose him.

She chose *him*. Call me, Fia. CALL ME. Tell me why.

I kick a pillow off my bed. "I'm sick of being useless."

"You aren't useless."

I laugh harshly. "Is that why you're so eager to ship me off?"

He doesn't respond. I think he's gone, so when he talks it startles me. "Fia wanted you safe."

"Yeah, well, Fia's not here, is she?" I stomp past him and out of the house. I've gone on enough walks to familiarize myself with the path down to the beach. It's late in the evening, the Georgia air still sticky, so there aren't many people out. I walk in relative silence, guided by the steady pulse of the ocean.

When I feel the ground shift into sand beneath my shoes, I take a few steps to the side and sit, facing the eternal ocean breeze. It doesn't smell like I thought it would. I spent too many years with those horrible "sea air" candles confusing my brain about what, exactly, a huge body of salt water would smell like. It's not sweet at all; it's heavy and cold with the slightest hint of decay.

But breathing it in, filling my lungs with it, makes me feel very, very alive.

Eden was from California. She always talked about taking me there and teaching me to surf. It wasn't until a year ago I found out she'd never surfed in her life; she'd lived in one of the interior desert cities and had never even seen the ocean.

If Fia wasn't going to stay with me, why couldn't she have gotten Eden out so I wouldn't have to be alone? Eden deserves the ocean.

Then again, Eden never hated the school like Fia always did and like I learned to. She'd laugh and say everything's relative. I can't imagine what her "relative" comparison was that the school was preferable, but I don't doubt it was horrible.

Someone sits next to me and I startle. "Sarah?"

"Cole."

I roll my eyes. I don't know why he's out here, but I'm not going to try and initiate conversation. I dig my hands into the sand, flashing back to that day on the beach in Chicago. That day I thought I knew exactly how everything would feel and turn out. That day they made my sister kill two people. I didn't see that. I never see enough.

I find a rock beneath the sand. Sarah told me they cart in the sand for the tourists, and that if you go a mile down the beach it's nothing but rocks. I rub my thumb along the contours of the stone, wonder how long it had to be turned around on the bottom of the ocean, battered and broken, until it came out this smooth.

"Why are you here?" I ask after a few minutes, unable to stand him sitting this close, saying nothing.

"I like the ocean."

I throw a handful of sand at him. "*Here* here, idiot. With Lerner. With Sarah. With Rafael. You don't seem to agree with anything they do, so why are you helping?"

My question is met with silence. I'm about ready to stand and go back to the house when he finally speaks. "My mom was psychic. She didn't talk about it much. I probably wouldn't have listened. I left home at fifteen. My father was . . . I shouldn't have left her there, but I was mad. Mad at him, but even angrier at her for staying. By the time I went back three years later, he was gone and she was sick." He pauses, the break punctuated by sharp laughing gulls. He clears his throat. "She forgave me. Told me to find a girl she'd been seeing in visions for months. One of Keane's."

"Sarah?" I've wondered about her. She knows so much that it wouldn't surprise me if she had worked for Keane at some point.

"No. Her name was Leanne. She was a Feeler."

For some reason it's a relief to me that Sarah never was Keane's. It makes her feel . . . cleaner. "Did you find her?"

"Too late. I don't know what they made her do, but she killed herself before I could get her out."

I let my head hang, feeling the weight of the memory on my shoulders. I reach out and find his arm, rest my hand there. "Fia tried . . . she tried to kill herself, too. It's not your fault. It's Keane's fault."

He clears his throat. "Sarah found me at my mom's funeral. I've been helping where I can ever since. I don't agree with all her decisions, especially not bringing in other people like Rafael, but someone has to do something." He sounds sad and lost, a quality in his voice I've never heard there before.

I squeeze his arm, then let my hand drop.

"Why did your sister go back?" he asks.

I curl up, resting my chin on my knees. "I honestly don't know. Maybe she wanted to stay with James." I glower, thinking about him. I hate him. "But who knows? Maybe she has some grand master plan." I snort, then move so my eyes are against my kneecaps, pushing into them. "Then again, planning was never her strong suit. She probably just felt like it."

"She loves you." He states it like fact.

"How do you know?" My eyes burn with tears, and I push them harder into my knees.

"When we took her, you were the only thing she cared about. She was desperate to get back to make sure you stayed safe."

I gasp a messy snort of a laugh. "I really thought she was going to kill me."

"And you still showed up."

"I owed Fia her freedom. And she needed me."

"As a general rule, when you think someone's going to kill you, you run the opposite direction."

"Yes, sir." I stand, brushing the sand off my pants. He joins me in the walk back to the house and I turn things around in my head, everything mixing together and jumbling up. Cole's tragic history. Fia's choice to leave me. Her relationship with James.

The world bursts into bright colors, and I see a girl, a teenager, but tiny. She's got white hair and black eyes. She's sitting across from a woman I actually recognize—Doris, from the school—but she looks bored, slouched with one leg draped lazily over the side of her chair.

"Could you please state your name?" Doris says, eyes narrowed thoughtfully.

The girl doesn't say anything, her gaze steady under one raised eyebrow.

Doris frowns. "Your name is not Katniss Everdeen. Think your name. Your name. The name your mother called you. The name on your birth certificate." Doris's face is growing angrier. "This isn't a joke."

"No, Doris Robertson, it isn't. But you are. This whole place is. Do any of you think I haven't already pulled from your brains exactly what's going on here? I don't want to talk to you. I want to talk to your boss. I should be working for Mr. Keane, not trapped in a school with a bunch of scared brats who have no idea what they can do. What's his phone number?"

Doris stammers. "I can't—you—"

The girl sighs and pulls out her phone, dialing a number. "Too easy," she says. "Hello, this is Mae Rubio. I'd like to speak with Mr. Keane."

The image shifts, and I see the same girl on a sidewalk, shivering, a wild and terrified look in her eyes. Another girl stands close, holding her by the arm. That's when I realize—Fia. She's with Fia. Whoever this girl is, she's going to be with Fia sometime in the future.

Fia's holding a broken bottle like a weapon.

And then I'm back in the dark, but not back in reality. I try not to freak out, try to calm my brain down because I'm worried if I get too excited the vision will stop, but it all continues as it did before. The hand in mine. The invisible slide and click of pieces falling into place as vision-me realizes she is in love.

"Annie," someone whispers, and I want to scream in frustration because if he's whispering, how can I recognize his voice when I hear it again? But vision-me, caught in the same eternal darkness I am, doesn't mind. She knows exactly who she is with and how she feels about it, and our racing hearts match pace.

"Annie?"

The sound of Cole's voice nearly makes my racing heart stop, until I realize with a shuddering gasp that reality has reclaimed me, and I'm back outside with Cole.

"Vision?"

I nod, disoriented. I'm sitting down. I wasn't sitting down before. "Did I fall?"

"You stopped walking and were pretty gone. I was worried you'd fall, so I helped you sit."

"Thanks." I push myself up, Cole's hand on my elbow turning me toward the house. I take off my sunglasses to rub the bridge of my nose, then settle them back into place.

"What did you see?" he asks, and it takes me a few seconds to process what he's asking. Visions are so disorienting. And I kind of resent having to dive back into reality *right now*; I'd like to hold on to the few remaining strands of how it felt to be me in that last vision. I love how it feels to be me in that vision. I want it so much it hurts.

"There you are," Rafael calls, his voice warm against the chill of the evening. I can hear his smile in it. "You left so quickly I was worried you were upset."

I shake my head. "No, I'm fine, I—"

"Did something happen? You look flushed." He puts his hand against my cheek, which means if I wasn't already flushed, I certainly am now.

"A vision."

"Really? Come, let's get you inside." He takes my hand—for the briefest second my heart flutters at the thought that it could be *his* hand—until I realize that it's not. I'd know that hand anywhere now, and it isn't Rafael's. There's a whisper of disappointment in my soul. It would have been so exciting to know it was Rafael. Oh well. He puts my hand on his arm, walking very close to me so that I'm entirely filled with the smell of him. The dark, heady spice of his cologne feels appropriate for how disoriented I am right now.

"There was a girl," I say, letting the images wash over my memory, relishing the look of the world. "White hair, dark eyes. At the school, being interviewed by a woman named Doris Robertson, a Reader there." I snort a small laugh. "The girl totally ran circles around her. Her name was . . . Mae Rubio.

And then later I saw her with Fia." I swallow hard against the swelling of emotions. "Not doing anything specific, but it looked like they knew each other. That's probably why I saw her in the first place." I don't mention the broken bottle or how scared Mae looked. Was Fia about to hurt her?

I feel sick thinking about it. I'm glad the vision ended when it did. For once I don't wish for more information.

"Explain?" Rafael prods. "Why would that make you see her?"

"Most of my visions involve Fia in one form or another. I'm the only person who can see her clearly." I realize maybe I should have told him this sooner, but I didn't want to talk about it. "She's so . . . umm, flighty? She's hard for Seers to grab ahold of. Clarice could never track her."

"Who is Clarice?"

I miss a step and he catches me around my waist. We're suddenly very, very close, but he doesn't let go or move away. Darn it, vision, couldn't it have been his hand? "She was my teacher. At the school. But she's dead."

"I see."

Cole's voice is like a rush of cold night air, bursting the bubble between Rafael and me. "We should find Mae. Talk to her before Keane gets her." I back up, embarrassed.

"I agree. And I think Annie should be the one to do it."

"What? Why?" Cole sounds suspicious.

"Who better to warn this poor girl of what her future holds than a beautiful woman who has escaped it?"

"You really think I should?" I ask.

"I do."

"Okay. I will." A smile pulls at my lips. I have something to do, and I'll be able to help, finally. I'll keep someone away from Keane. I'll save a girl from the school. Fia would be proud.

FIA

Two Days Before

I COULD WALK STRAIGHT BACK. HE'S IN THERE—PAST THAT doorway, somewhere in the maze of offices in this gleaming, window-lit skyscraper. Walk straight back. I don't know what I'd do when I got there. Probably nothing that works with the plan. But my fingers itch to *do.*

"Don't," Pixie says, not looking up from her magazine. She's manning the front desk, and I'm sitting on top of it. I'm just *sitting* here.

She glares up at me. "You're not sitting, you're lurking. And you wouldn't get very far. There's a buttload of security guards once you get past that door, and you're on the watch list. So you can't go back and see James."

James. Yes. I was thinking about *James.* Of course that's what

I was thinking about. I want to go back to see James. I want to jump him, throw him across a desk, rip off his shirt and . . .

"SHUT UP, gag, you are so gross."

I smile and tap my temple, but that was close. I have to be more careful. James asked me again this morning for a verdict he could give his father.

I don't know if I'm delaying because I like Pixie and worry what will happen to her, or if I'm delaying because I'm worried about whatever job his father would have for me next. But I'll have to decide soon. Decide what to do with Pixie. Pick her fate. I reach out and brush her bangs out of her eyes.

She doesn't look up. "Did you figure out who was watching you?" she asks, slowly tearing strips through the glowingly photoshopped face of some pop star.

"Hmm?" I jump off the desk and walk to one of the floor-to-ceiling windows. I can see the green beacon of Central Park from here. It'd be nice to be down there today. But I need to be here. Why? I can't do anything right now. I feel like I need to be here, though.

"Last night, before you left with James. Remember? At the club?"

I shrug. "No idea." I hadn't even thought about it. Last night James held me and we laughed, and we dared to talk about a plan, our plan, and a future without all this. Whatever was happening at the club is yet another thing on my endless list of things to worry about or not worry about. I opt not to worry. Why worry about something as stupid as that? If I have to confront it, I will. And I'll win.

Tap tap tap tap. I win.

"You want to do something tonight? Or do you have plans with Peachy Keane?"

James would hate that nickname. I'll have to use it. I feel a little better today. More patient. I roll my eyes, the word sticking in my head like one of my taps. Awful word.

The main office door opens and a woman walks in. "Afternoon," she says, her voice low and sleepy.

Pixie pops her gum loudly, then pushes a button under her desk that opens the door to the hall. The woman goes straight back.

"We should see a movie. Movies are quiet. People don't think much during them." Pixie's voice buzzes at me, but I can't quite focus on it.

Something.

Something.

Something.

Something is wrong. Very wrong. SO WRONG.

I whirl around just in time to see the door close behind the woman. "What was she thinking?"

Pixie sees my expression and frowns. "I don't know, paperwork deadlines. Her thoughts are never interesting."

"Let me back."

"Fia, I can't—"

I jump over the desk, knock her down, and push the button. The doors click unlocked and I throw them open, sprint through. A guard stands up from his chair and sputters something, blocking my way. I punch him in the neck and keep going.

Around the corner. Everything is buzzing, every internal alarm ringing, I feel sick and I feel tight and coiled like a spring. I see the back of the woman as she opens a plain door and walks in.

Wrong.

"You can't be back here," a man says, roughly grabbing my elbow. I put a foot against the wall and use it for leverage, shoving myself into him. He's off-balance. I drop to the floor and sweep his legs, knocking him down.

Can't stop. Can't wait.

More footsteps pounding behind me but I don't care, I throw myself at the door, slam through.

Everything is fuzzy, the room out of focus except the woman. Her back is to me but she is in sharp relief, every line clear, every instinct in my body tuned in to her.

Stop stop stop stop her, I have to stop her! I lower my shoulder and run straight forward, slamming her head into the edge of a table with a resounding crack. She collapses on the floor and I pin her arm behind her back.

My heart races, but everything else starts to calm, the rush in my ears fading and my vision going back to normal. She looks small and fragile there on the carpet, wearing a white blouse and charcoal dress slacks. Her hair is still perfectly set in a bun at the base of her neck and I—

Oh, no, please no, please no no I didn't mean to I didn't want to—

I see her chest move and I lean back, exhaling with relief. She's not dead.

I'm grabbed roughly from behind. Elbow to the nose, turn, knee to the crotch, I am a fury of fists and knees and elbows, but there are a lot of them. I don't know why I'm fighting them, I don't need to fight them except they won't leave me alone.

They have stun guns. Now I *want* to fight them. I break a nose, pop an arm out of its socket, fight my way into the corner. Two left. Two on one. Not fair.

Not a problem.

"Stop! Get off her!" James shouts.

The security guard immediately in front of me pauses. I slam my head into his nose and he stumbles backward, clutching it.

Good. Now no one is touching me. I don't want anyone to touch me. I smooth down the front of my black tee, then finally take in the room. Several men in various stages of shock sit around a large oval table. The table I slammed the woman into.

She's still lying on the floor, but James is crouching next to her.

"She's not dead," I blurt, needing to say it and needing him to confirm it. "I didn't kill her."

James finally looks up and meets my eyes. I can read the panic hidden there, but his face is carefully composed. "She's unconscious."

"Why did you attack her?" a handsome older man with salt-and-pepper hair asks, and when I look at him I feel

nothing

nothing

nothing

so much nothing I worry that I will lose myself in it.

I shake my head, trying to snap out of it. He is worse than the distraction of the wrong feeling. There is something so strong in the way I react to him that it goes beyond right or wrong. I can hardly breathe. "I needed to."

"She's worked here for five years."

James stands, holding a handgun. "She had this. I think Fia saved your life."

The man's expression doesn't change. He doesn't have an expression. He's not a person. For the first time in my life I think I know what fear—true fear—feels like. Because everything about him is off, so far off I don't even know how to process it.

"Aren't you going to introduce us?" he says, and I think he is smiling, but it isn't a smile because he isn't a person. My instincts made me run in here, my instincts made me stop whatever this woman was going to do. But this man can't be right, can't be.

James sets the gun on the table. "Fia, this is my father, Phillip Keane."

I smile because there is no other option. It is all I can do to hold in a burst of laughter, because this is the funniest thing that has ever happened to me and I am broken, once and for all, completely broken.

I just saved the life of the man I've vowed to destroy.

ANNIE

Two and a Half Months Before

"FIA," I MUTTER, STOMPING INTO MY ROOM AND throwing open my closet door. "You'd better be having the time of your life to make up for abandoning me and forcing me to figure this all out on my own."

When I agreed to talk to Mae, I didn't realize they'd track her down within a day. I wanted to be useful, I did, I *do*, but this feels fast. I'm not sure what to say to save this girl. But it should work out, shouldn't it? Since I'm doing the right thing?

There is the tiniest hint of an exhalation in the room and I spin around, clutching my things to my chest. "Who's there?"

No one answers.

My heart racing, I edge toward the door. Now that I'm listening I can hear all the little sounds a body makes when it is trying its hardest to be silent. I open my mouth to scream, but . . . I know everyone in this house. I'm not going to be scared in my own room.

I plaster a smile on my face and shake my head. "You're going crazy, Annie." I let my shoulders relax, hum, and toss my clothes toward the bed, then walk out into the hall and close the door behind myself.

I count to twenty, then throw the door open and scream "GOTCHA!"

I'm answered by a shriek. A guy's shriek. "*Adam?*"

"I'm so sorry," he says. "I didn't mean to— You came in, and I didn't want you to know—I was looking for something but then it was too late to let you know I was in here, and then once I was quiet for a few seconds, it felt too weird to suddenly announce myself, and . . . I am so, so sorry."

I frown. This is unlike him. He always lets me know when he comes into or leaves a room. "What were you looking for?"

"Umm. The phone. I was checking the phone. Rafael found a lab for me, so I won't be here when you get back. I wanted to make sure we hadn't missed any contact from Fia."

I walk and sit down on the edge of my bed. "You could have asked."

"Are you sure there's no other way she might try to contact us? Email? Anything?"

"I would tell you if there were."

He exhales heavily. "I thought she'd be back by now. I'm worried."

My heart feels heavy in my chest. All Adam's careful attention, all his kindness. He's been good company, but now I know it has nothing to do with me. It's about Fia. Everything always is, even when she is nowhere near, even when she left all of us. We still orbit the brilliant, chaotic burning of her star.

"You really care about my sister, don't you?" I don't want him to. He's so sweet. I can't imagine anyone loving Fia without being hurt by it.

I love her more than anyone, and it's killing me.

He sits next to me. "I lost everything and everyone. I haven't even been able to contact my family. They think I'm dead, Annie. My mom, I can't even imagine . . ." His voice breaks, and I reach out for his hand. It's not, I note with no small amount of relief, the hand from my visions. "Fia's the reason I'm here, and I can't believe that there isn't a purpose behind it all. Not with what I've seen, not with what you all can do. There has to be a reason we met. A reason that makes everything worthwhile."

I'm the reason they met. Not fate. I created this future with my stupid reaction to my visions. But I don't think Adam would see it that way. Clinical, brilliantly medical-minded Adam believes in fate. A fate with Fia.

"We change the future with every choice we make," I say

softly. I don't know whether I mean it to encourage or discourage the torch he carries for my sister.

Something thuds outside the bathroom. I leave the shower running but climb out, curious. The stone tiles are cold under my feet as I pad across them and put my ear against the door.

"If you so much as look in her direction again, I'll kill you." Cole. He insisted on coming with me to North Carolina on the Mae trip, so Rafael sent him and Nathan. It was the most awkward car trip in the history of car trips: Nathan with his terrible choice in music, Cole silent and fuming.

Nathan answers. "Relax! I was just in here for—"

"I've seen you watching her when you think no one notices. One more time—" Something thuds against the wall and I jump back, nearly slipping on the tiles. "One more time and I'll break your neck."

Well then. Horrified, I climb back into the shower.

After my hair is dry, I dress in the bathroom, now hyperaware of who might be hanging around my room in the hotel suite unobserved. At least I can smell Nathan coming from several rooms away. Sure enough, as I walk out into my bedroom the sharp stinging stink of him lingers.

The television is on, too. "Hello?" I say.

"It's me," Cole answers.

"And if I had walked out naked?"

"My eyes are closed. Can I open them now?"

I walk to the bench at the foot of the bed and sit down. "Yes. Why are you in my room?"

"Bored."

"So, slamming Nathan into the wall isn't enough to keep you entertained for a few minutes?"

"Ah." He makes a small, regretful noise with his mouth. "You heard that. Sarah says I don't play well with other boys. Oh, your phone kept beeping while you were in the shower."

My heart skips a beat—what if it was Fia?—but I try to sound casual. "Who is it? You can check, I don't mind."

Cole gets up and then says, "Adam. Five texts. I can read them to you." He pauses. "Unless they're personal."

I roll my eyes. "Not that it's any of your business, but I'm pretty sure he's desperately in love with my sister."

Cole snorts. "He's crazy."

"He'd have to be, right?" I stop, horrified with myself. Cole bursts out with a shockingly staccato laugh and then I can't help but laugh, too. Maybe it's betraying Fia, I don't know, but it feels good to be able to laugh about her with someone who knows her, or at least has met her. Makes me feel less alone.

I twist my hair up into a bun, a smile lingering on my face. "Oh, speaking of crazy, do I need to be concerned about Nathan?"

"No."

"Because you're watching him?"

"Because if he tries anything, you can handle yourself."

I jerk my knee up, then pantomime grabbing my groin and falling to the floor in pain. I'm rewarded with another bark of laughter.

Pushing myself up, I sit on the floor and pull out my hair, redo it. "Did Rafael call?"

When Cole says Rafael's name, it sounds like he's bitten into something bitter and wants to spit it out. "No, Rafael didn't call. But Mae works at a restaurant and has a shift this afternoon. It might be an easy way to meet her and establish contact—less threatening than showing up at her house."

"It's a plan. You coming with me?"

"I think it'd be better for you to be alone, but I'll be close by."

"Fair enough." I can handle this. I can.

But by the time he drops me off at the café I'm a raging bundle of nerves.

I sit in a booth, nervously tapping on my plate until I'm hit with a sudden longing for Fia. I adjust my sunglasses, then fold my hands in my lap.

I put my elbow on the table and lean my chin against it. *Mae, Mae, Mae,* I think. *Where are you, Mae? I want to talk to you.* I feel like an idiot, sending out thoughts to the café when I have no idea if she's even here. What if she didn't show up for her shift today? What if it's the wrong Mae Rubio?

Someone sits across from me with a huff. "Will you stop it? You're giving me a headache with all that shouting. It's creepy."

I sit up straight and smile. "Mae?"

"No, the other mind reader you've been screaming at for the last thirty minutes of my shift. What's your problem? And how do you know about me?" She sounds young, but with a hard edge.

"I'm Amy." I hold my hand out straight, but she ignores it, so I drop it and fiddle with my cutlery.

"Wonderful, *Amy*. That explains everything."

"I know about you because I work for a group dedicated to protecting women like us."

"Like us?" She's quiet for a little bit, then she snorts. "No reaction. Obviously you are not like me."

"No, not exactly. I'm not a Reader, I'm a Seer. I see things before they happen."

I gasp as a glass of ice water is thrown in my face.

Mae laughs. "Guess you didn't see that coming."

I fumble for my napkin, knocking a spoon or fork off the table with a metallic clatter that makes me cringe. "It doesn't work like that. I don't see *everything* before it happens, just like you don't hear every thought anyone ever has."

"Pretty close," she says, and I'm surprised to hear a tinge of—sadness? Wistfulness? "Though I can't figure you out. You haven't had one snarky thought about me. Most straight girls think mean things the second they see me. You aren't going to comment on my hair or my clothes? What about my boobs? No boob judgery? What are you, a robot?"

I push my sunglasses to the top of my head. "I tend not to care what people look like."

"Oh." She sounds deflated. "Sorry." She sips, and then a cup clinks down. "So, what are you doing here?"

"You're going to get—or may have already gotten—an offer to go to a special school for girls. You should know what you're dealing with."

I lean back and think—details, the few insights I have from visions, memories. The night I overheard the teachers talking about how to keep various girls under control. The bruises all over Fia's body I didn't know about until Eden told me. When Mr. Keane personally threatened to kill me if I messed up.

He would have done it. Still would, given the chance. I have no doubt.

Mae lets out a long breath. "Well. That was a lot of information."

"They've already trapped too many girls, stolen too many futures." I wait expectantly for her to ask how to get away from Keane and stay unnoticed.

"How do they get girls to do it? They're targeting psychics and mind readers. How do they fool them into working for them?"

I frown, taken aback. I hadn't planned on getting into this much explanation. Cole said to scare her away. "Well, not everyone is as skilled as you. I had no idea anything was wrong with the school for years." Fia always knew. I should have paid more attention. They'd destroyed her before I even figured out I should worry. "It's not like they start out most girls with assassinations. It's little things. And they pay really well."

"Oh?"

"Yeah. At least that's what I heard. The school is prestigious. My aunt was thrilled to send us. And then they set up the girls who are talented enough with jobs. But they own you. You can't get out. Mr. Keane, the man in charge of everything, is pretty patently evil."

"What's the point of it all?"

"I don't know the endgame. I only know details. He's got eyes and ears in a lot of things. I think he wants power and control, and he uses and manipulates a lot of people to get it."

"Hmm. And Fia? Where is she now that you can't go three thoughts without missing her? Dead?"

"I . . ." My stomach drops. Oh no, what have I done? Cole said to stay anonymous, and here I've already shown her that I'm a blind psychic connected to Fia. How many of those are there walking around?

"Yeah, you aren't very good at this." She laughs and I put a hand over my mouth, horrified. "Relax, 'Amy' the Blind Psychic. I've been around the block. You learn about people pretty quickly when you can listen in on the stuff they don't filter. You're a good person and you really think you're doing me a favor by warning me about this sinister organization that wants to use my powers for eeeeevvvvviiiiillll." She pauses. "I was stroking an imaginary beard when I said that, just so you know. Answer me this: Why is Fia still working for them?"

My shoulders slump. "I honestly don't know."

"I think I understand," Mae says, her voice soft. "Because here's where you're wrong. You're treating all these women as victims, unable to get out of this crazy trap. But can't you see that *we're the ones with all the power*?"

"You don't know what they're like, what they'll do to control you."

"No, I can imagine. But if they're willing to go that far to use us, it makes me think they're scared silly that someone else will beat them at their own game. And I like that. I think Fia figured it out, too. Plus, to be honest, I kind of dig the idea of being showered with money and power for something I can do in my sleep."

"But—"

"No buts. I'm not a victim and I'm not going to let a corporation turn me into one. Girls like you and me? We hold all the cards. We just have to be smart enough to see it."

"You're going to say yes to them," I whisper. How could I have messed this up so bad?

"Don't worry. Your secret is safe with me. We never met."

I reach across the table, find her hand, squeeze it in mine. I should be screaming at her, telling her to do anything else, but the vision of her sticks in my head. Now I wish I knew how it ended. "My real name is Annie. I'm dead. Will you watch out for her? Fia? She's so alone. I can't—I hate that I can't be there for her. I don't care why she's still with them. I just want her to be happy and safe. But be careful. She can be . . . dangerous."

Mae squeezes my hand back. Her voice is softer, kinder. "Okay. I think she and I will get along really well."

I laugh, letting go and sitting back, suddenly exhausted. "You're certainly both crazy enough."

I hear her stand. "Good luck, Annie."

Did I mess this up? Could I have changed her mind? Fia could have. Fia would have known exactly what to do, what to say, heck, what to *think*. I messed everything up. But a small part of me is hopeful that maybe I'm sending a friend Fia's way.

Please, please let me not have sent Mae into even more danger by putting her onto Fia's path.

"Good luck, Mae." *You're going to need it.*

She laughs brightly. "I make my luck. I pull it out of the brains of everyone I meet."

A few minutes later someone else sits across from me. "How did it go?" Cole asks.

"I was brilliant. Anyone else you want me to drive straight into Keane's employ?"

"What do you mean?"

"I—" A familiar voice asking for a table for one registers and I freeze. It's a man. How do I know his voice? "Crap," I hiss, ducking and crawling on the floor until I'm under the table.

"What are you doing?" Cole asks.

"Shut up!" I hiss. "There's a man here. He's a recruiter for the school. If he sees me, I'm dead." *Actually* dead, as opposed to fictionally dead.

"What does he look like?"

I punch Cole's thigh so hard my hand stings.

"Sorry! Sorry. There's a guy in a suit by himself. He's watching Mae. I think it's him. We'll wait it out."

I sit with my back against the wall, knees bumping his, head craned at a horrible angle beneath the table. Cole orders food, acting casual.

"This is why I wanted you gone," he says, voice so low I can barely hear it over the hum of conversations and the clinking of silverware.

"Because I screw everything up?"

"Because sending you on a collision course with Keane is the worst possible thing we can do."

My aching neck agrees with him. I have to figure out a way to be better. This was not enough.

I was not enough.

FIA

Thirty-six Hours Before

~

I PLAY IT OVER AND OVER AGAIN IN MY HEAD, TRYING to unstick whatever got stuck and made me do something so stupid.

She walked by. I knew I needed to stop her.

I *knew* I needed to stop her. There was no doubt. I have so much doubt these days, but there was no doubt then.

I tap tap tap tap on my stomach, the polished oval table I'm lying on hard beneath the back of my head and the base of my spine. The chandelier overhead, understated and elegantly modern, burns funny patterns of light on my eyes. The sun has long since gone down, but no one has bothered coming in, telling me I can go or I can stay or anything.

I saved his life. Saved it so I can destroy it? Wouldn't everything be better if he were dead now? And I wouldn't even have had to be the one to do it.

Someone opens the door and walks into the empty conference room James left me in with a caution not to go anywhere. I don't look over. I'm too busy tap tap tap tapping, trying to puzzle out the *why* of all this.

"Sedatives," Pixie says, matter-of-factly. "Apparently she's been taking massive doses of sedatives for the last few weeks to get by all the Feeler check-ins. No wonder her thoughts were so sleepy."

She walked by. She needed to be stopped. Why? Why did she need to be stopped? "It was Mr. Keane, right? She was there to kill him. Not James or someone else." Maybe she was going to kill James. It would be right for me to stop that. I would need to stop that, because I need James.

Pixie sits on the table next to me. "Yup. Kill order for El Presidente. No one else, as far as I could tell. They had me pull what I could from her thoughts, but she was pretty good."

Pixie isn't telling me everything. She got more than that. I need to know what else she got. Don't think about it.

I saved him. The man who destroyed me. The man who would have hurt Annie, done anything, to control me. Saving him was the *right* thing to do.

I laugh so hard I have to wipe the tears away from where they trace down the corners of my eyes and tunnel into my hair. "So

I really did save his life." Spinning and spinning and landing on this. This?

"You really did." Pixie leans into my field of vision, eyebrows knit. "You okay in there?"

"What are they doing with the woman?"

"Casey? I didn't ask."

I sit up. Suddenly Pixie is very intent on avoiding my eyes. "You don't *have* to ask. What are they doing with her?"

Pixie shrugs, tugs on the bar piercing her lower lip. "Women who cross him end up overdosing. Every time. It's a strange coincidence, how they all overdose and die."

Sarah saw that. Did she see Casey? Was that one of the faces that drove her to . . .

"Who is Sarah?"

I glare at Pixie, then shrug. "Someone I used to know."

Tap tap tap tap. I didn't kill Casey. I didn't. Not my fault. Not my problem. I did what I was supposed to. She's not mine. If I hadn't stopped her, she would have killed Mr. Keane. Would I have blamed myself for that death? Do I want that death?

"Wanna go dancing?" I ask.

"Hells yes."

Pixie shrugs into her leather coat and we walk together toward the lobby. The lobby I was so desperate to get past this morning. Will I be stuck there again? Mr. Keane is nowhere to be seen, but we pass an open door and I look in to see James listening as two other men talk. He's pale, obviously troubled by today's events, but gives me a ghost of a smile and a hint of a nod.

Guess I did something right after all. I don't think access will be a problem again.

All it took was foiling one murder and causing another.

I drag Pixie onto the dance floor with me, try to help her forget everything, turn it off, stop listening. She whines that she can't stop hearing things.

"Let it be static," I say. "Don't tune in."

I also give her drinks stronger than Shirley Temples. A lot of them. I tip my own drinks back and think how buzzed I am getting, how I really shouldn't have any more to drink but, hey, why not.

Meanwhile, I don't actually drink anything.

I smile at Pixie as she nods her head in time to the music. Or rather, not actually at all in time to the music. Her eyelids droop and she sways into my shoulder, resting her head there. Sleepy drunk. Sleepy drunks are adorable. Angry drunks are less so. Funnier, though.

"So," I say. "Are you loyal to Mr. Keane?"

"I am loyal to myself. Whatever gets me where I want to go."

"And right now?"

"Right now that's my big fat paychecks."

At least I can tell James she's cleared for loyalty. It makes me sad. But, then again, I'm here, doing bad things, because I am trying to get to where I want to go.

But I lost where that was. I can't find it anymore. I saved his life. That can't have been right. There is no world in which sacrificing that woman for Mr. Keane is right. And if I can't feel right anymore . . .

I poke Pixie to make sure she's still awake. "The crazy woman was plotting to kill Mr. Keane. How long do you think she was working toward it?"

"Casey. Her name was Casey. And she's planned it for months."

"By herself?"

Pixie shakes her head. "No. She thought of a few other names."

"And they were?"

"Lerner. That's the one I told them. She also thought about James."

I frown. "Well, she knows him, obviously."

"It didn't feel like that kind of thinking about him. But I didn't mention that."

"You didn't?" She isn't totally loyal, then? Does she keep things from Keane?

"Of course I don't tell them everything," she says. The tears pooling in her eyes catch the light, glinting more than the studs in her eyebrow. "Is it our fault? That she's going to die?"

I shake my head. Then I shrug. "Her fault. She got caught."

"Because of us." Pixie looks like her heart is breaking, and I know what that feels like, how deep those fissures go, how much of your soul cracks off and disappears.

"No. Look at me. Look at me, Pixie. You wouldn't have caught her. I did. You have no blame in this. Understand?"

She shakes her head, so I grab her chin and force her face up, right next to mine. "This is not your fault. Say it."

She hiccups a sob, then nods. "This is not my fault."

"Good." I lean back against the bench, pull her so her head is nestled between my neck and my shoulder. She's so young. So young.

"I'm only two years younger than you. You can trust me, you know."

I laugh. I trust no one and no one trusts me. Not even James. I know he hides things from me, but I let him, because it's the only way to make things work.

"There was another name the woman thought. I didn't tell them."

"What?" I whisper, my stomach clenching with that roller-coaster anticipation of falling. Bad. This is bad.

"Annie."

No. No no no no. NO NO NO NO. ANNIE IS DEAD. ANNIE IS DEAD. ANNIE IS DEAD I KILLED HER I KILLED HER I KILLED HER SHE'S DEAD.

Pixie sits up and looks at me, trying to smile, but holding her head like it's in pain. "It's okay. I met her a couple months ago. She's okay, Fia. No one knows. She asked me to keep an eye out for you."

My thoughts are frozen with shock. Pixie met Annie. And she's never let it slip. "Because Annie is dead. No one knows because *she is dead*." I watch Pixie, every sense trained on her for her reaction.

She nods, slowly, solemnly. "Yes. I know. Annie is dead."

"And she stays dead." *Or I'll kill you. I will, I will. You wouldn't be the first person I killed to protect her. Or even the second.*

Her shoulders fall and she looks hurt. "You don't have to do that. I wouldn't. We're friends. Aren't we?" She stands and stumbles away from me.

I swear under my breath. How can I keep her quiet? She can't know about Annie. That isn't safe. I have to keep Annie safe.

Whatever it takes.

I chase after her, grabbing her arm, my beer bottle still clutched in my other hand. "Listen, Pixie, I'm sorry. You have to understand—"

"Run," she says.

"What?"

"Run! They're thinking your name! All of them! Too many of them!"

I look up, around the room, dark and filled with bodies,

packed with them. And then I realize that the fear I felt, still feel, the warning, had nothing to do with Pixie. I have no weapons on me, and I lost my security tail on the way here as a matter of habit.

"He wants you unharmed," Pixie whispers, her lips against my ear. I have my arm around her waist as I steer her toward the main exit. Our best bet is a crowd. They've already seen us, so sneaking out the back would only work to their advantage. "Do you know someone named Rafael?"

I clench my jaw against the flood of memories. Rafael on a beach in Greece. Rafael's lips on mine in my first kiss. Rafael's hands all over me. Rafael's unknown score to settle with James. This is bad.

Then again, I still owe him for that kiss. I smash the bottom off my bottle to leave a jagged edge.

Time to meet an old friend.

ANNIE

Nine Weeks Before

I SLAM THE DOOR, SLUMPING IN THE PASSENGER SEAT while Cole loads the grocery bags.

When he gets in, he doesn't start the car. "What's wrong?"

"What do you think?" I fold my arms, scowling.

"Look, you did your best. No reason to feel sorry."

"Really? Then why is it that in the last week since I failed with Mae, I've done nothing except sit around the house? Adam's off to do fancy research, Sarah's in and out, Rafael's gone, you're not here most of the time. Everyone else is busy, and I'm lucky if I get to make a grocery run."

"What do you want to do?"

"Help!"

"Annie, no one would have recognized that man as being from Keane. If anyone else had been sent to contact Mae, they would have been caught. Probably killed. If you hadn't been paying attention, you would have been snatched. And Fia would have been in trouble, too, for lying about killing you. It's not worth risking that."

"Fia would be fine," I mutter, putting my feet up on the dash. "She always figures it out."

"I don't blame you for what happened with Mae."

"Really? Because I blame me."

"She had a choice, and she made the wrong one. But you gave her options. No one did that for you."

"That's not true. Fia told me not to go to the school, and I didn't listen."

"Again, not your fault."

I rub my forehead, the beginnings of a headache pulsing behind my eyes. I haven't had so much as a hint of a vision since the one with Mae. Maybe my own brain has decided I'm worthless, too.

"I was thinking," he says. "If you wanted to learn some self-defense, I'd be happy to teach you."

"What good will that do?"

"More than you think. We'd play to your strengths."

"In case you haven't been paying attention, I'm a scrawny blind girl."

"Exactly. Let other people underestimate you, and then use that to your advantage."

"So basically you're saying my strength is that I have no strengths."

His staccato laugh rings through the car and I smile in spite of myself.

"Okay, fine," I say. "You can teach me some things. After tea. I need some tea like nobody's business."

He pulls to a stop. I get out of the car and try to decide what kind of tea day today is while he gets the bags.

"Looks like Rafael is here," Cole says, not sounding particularly enthused. I, on the other hand, have missed the sexy sounds of Rafael's voice. Nobody reads a menu like him. I can't help but feel a little giddy knowing I'll get to hang out with him. It's just mindless flirting—curse his not-right hands—but a little mindless flirting makes me feel real and normal in the most comforting way.

"I hope he brought Sarah!" I hurry up the stairs and throw open the door. "Hey," I call. "Who's back?"

I take a few steps, then the groceries drop to the floor with a shattering of glass jars as Cole grabs me and shoves me to the closed door. His back presses against me, blocking my whole body. "What the—"

That's when the unfamiliar but instantly recognizable sound of a gun being cocked fills the air. "Well now," says a voice I never expected to hear again. The phantom smell of mustard and the memory of a thousand times walking past him overcomes me.

Hallway Darren. "You look good for being dead, Annie. Come on in."

Cole takes my arm, keeping me behind him as we walk forward slowly. Then Cole is roughly pulled away. I hear him pushed to the floor, a low grunt his only protest.

"Don't bother with this one." Hallway Darren shoves me onto the couch. "She's not any trouble without her sister. Finish tying him up and put him next to the other guy." He must be talking about Rafael.

"I got it," another man says.

"Anyone else in the house? I'll know if you're lying." A woman, speaking from across the room. I don't know if she's a Reader or a Feeler, but either way, we're screwed.

My heart races and I'm overcome with despair. This was all for nothing. If I go back, I am as good as dead. I hang my head, letting the fear wash over me, radiate out. I concentrate on feeling that, and that alone. I don't let myself think anything.

"There's no one else," Sarah says. She sounds like she's on the couch, too. Darren and the other man are directly in front of me. The woman is near the kitchen. Cole is . . .

"Don't move," the other man says, and I hear someone get pushed against the wall. Okay. Cole and Rafael must be near the sliding glass door to the patio.

I am worthless. I am less than worthless. I can't do anything.

"She's not lying," the woman says. "This is everyone. Want

me to figure out who those two are?"

"Nah, only the girls matter." Darren sounds positively gleeful. "I can't believe Annie's alive. I'd better call this one in right now."

Without thinking, I lunge forward, head ducked. My shoulder slams into Darren's stomach and I throw my arms around his waist and push. We fall to the ground together; I sink my teeth into his bicep and scramble to find his hand.

The side of the gun connects with my head, and everything explodes in brilliant pain. Dazed, I grab for his gun, but he flips me off and onto my stomach, his knee digging into my back.

A loud pop, followed by another.

I brace myself for the pain, but it doesn't come. Instead the pressure on my back disappears and Darren falls onto my arm. I jerk it out from under him and scramble away.

"It's all right," Cole says, putting his tied-together hands on my shoulder. "They're down."

Rafael speaks for the first time. "Are you okay, Casey?"

The woman takes a shuddering breath. "Yeah. Thanks."

"What just happened?" Sarah asks. "Who are you?"

"I'm sorry," Casey says. "I tried to warn you we were coming, but I was never alone."

"Casey's been working with me for months," Rafael explains. "She's in deep at Keane."

I try to stand but am shaking too much, so I sit where I am.

Cole talks from the kitchen, where I hear a soft snicking sound that I assume is him, cutting his wrists free. "How did they find us?"

I am sitting in a room with two dead men. I hate this. I want to be anywhere else.

The woman, Casey, sits on the couch. "Keane's got a Seer trained on you, Rafael. You've got to be more careful."

Rafael sounds tired. "Okay. Does James know his father sent them after me?"

"I don't think so. This one was secret. That's why I couldn't contact you—they took my cell away and didn't even tell me where we were going until we were here."

"But no one knows Annie is alive, right?" Sarah asks.

"Besides her." I nod in Casey's general direction.

"Secret is safe with me. The Seer only saw Rafael—good thing you weren't together at the time. Well, I'm gonna have to request that someone shoot me."

"What?" Sarah asks, her voice strangled.

"I can't lose their trust now. The story is, we were ambushed, Darren and Mark were fatally shot, and I got away after being shot in the arm." She takes a deep breath, whispering either a prayer or a curse to God.

I shake my head. "This is ridiculous. You don't have to get shot. You were waiting outside in the car while they cleared the house. You heard the shots, saw someone run out with a gun, and drove away. All we have to do is shoot a couple of holes in the car."

"Oh, I like that idea so much better," Casey says.

"On it." Cole walks out the front door.

"What about the bodies?" Sarah whispers, and I am so glad I can't see what she can. I crawl across the floor to the couch, then sit and put my arm around her shoulder. She leans into me. My head still hurts where Darren hit it with the gun.

Darren's dead now.

"Call Nathan," Rafael says. "Tell him what happened. This house is officially closed, but he can come clean up."

Sarah squeezes my hand, then stands and walks out of the room, her voice trailing away as she gives directions over the phone.

I shake my head, overwhelmed and tired. And then I realize that I don't feel guilty. Darren and the other man wouldn't have been shot if I hadn't tackled him and given Casey an opening. I'm entirely culpable in their deaths.

"I'm confused, too," Casey says.

"Feeler?"

"Yup."

"Shouldn't I feel guilty?" I remember how devastated Fia was after helping with the package bomb that killed two people. How hollow she was after killing Clarice. I just feel . . . tired. And a little bit relieved. No one I care about died today.

"I don't think there's any way you should or shouldn't feel right now. I don't know how to feel, either." The couch squeaks as she leans forward. "Wow, I am so not looking forward to going back to work."

"What are you doing there?"

"The usual. Human resources. Light espionage. I mostly interview employees as a human lie detector. It's my specialty."

"No, I mean for Rafael."

"That I can't tell you. I can't even let myself think about it. I'll have to move faster now, though."

I nod, understanding. "Word of advice: don't ever plan ahead."

"Yeah, rotten Seers. No offense. But thanks. Your quick thinking back there saved everyone."

I nod, not really sure a "you're welcome" is appropriate with two dead men on the floor.

The front door opens. "Done," Cole says.

"I'm off then, on my mad getaway from gun-toting brigands. Wish me luck." She tries for perky on that last sentence, but it sounds wistful and sad.

"Good luck," I whisper as the door closes behind her.

"We need to get out of here now. Everybody pack," Rafael says.

I stand and walk up to my room. So much for being bored. I grab my electronics and throw them in the bag I always keep packed with my fake documents. Shove some clothes in on top of them. I don't have much stuff.

"Do you need help?" Rafael asks from the doorway.

I lean against my closet. "No. I don't know. I should have seen this coming."

"Everyone is safe. That's what's important."

I shake my head. "I'm tired of being safe and protected. I want to do something. Give me Adderall."

"What?"

"I know Sarah's taking it to give herself a boost. I want it, too. I'm the only one who can see Fia, right? But what good does that do if I never see anything? I need to see more."

"I'm not sure this is a good idea."

"I want it. I'll get it whether or not you help me." I have no idea how to begin to go about getting drugs illegally. But I hope I sound convincing.

He sighs. "Fine. When we're safely away from here, I'll get some for you. But we'll be careful."

I nod, but it's a lie. I don't care about being careful. I care about being useful. And I'll do anything to make that happen.

FIA

Thirty-two Hours Before

THERE ARE TOO MANY. THIS IS OBVIOUS. TAP TAP TAP tap the broken bottle's flat side against my leg. My free hand is on Pixie's arm, holding her close to my body. I edge us out the main doors and onto the sidewalk, but everything here is noisy and fast and I don't know how to do this.

Hmm. It's a puzzle.

Something hard jabs into my back. "I've got a gun on you. Try anything and I'll shoot."

I turn around, face-to-face with a short, stocky man. "I hate it when people threaten to shoot me. Either shoot me or don't, but stop talking about it. Besides, you aren't supposed to hurt me."

I feel the twinge of error a split second before his eyes shift to tiny Pixie next to me. A smile creeps across his blocky features and he moves the gun hidden in his jacket pocket toward her. "I'll shoot your girlfriend."

Pixie would be dead, and it wouldn't be by my hand. Annie's secret would be safe again.

No. I can't—won't—let her die. It would be easier, but it isn't right. I spin behind him, pulling him against my body and shoving the jagged edge of the glass against his neck. "Get that gun away from her."

He starts to move, so I push harder. "You'll bleed to death before you get to the hospital."

"You should listen to her," Pixie babbles, whites showing all around her irises, which are fixed on the outline of the gun. "She's never wrong."

"If you hurt me, there are more of us, they'll shoot her. It won't matter if you kill me."

"But it matters to you, doesn't it?" I rest my chin on the back of his neck. He smells like floral shampoo and terror. "Here's what we're going to do. You're going to let Pixie hail a cab and get in. As soon as she is safely in the car and gone, I'll come with you, no problem."

"How do I know you're telling the truth?"

I dig the glass in, because he's annoying me and I'm jittery and anxious to see Pixie safely off. They can't hurt her. I won't let them. I need Pixie secure even though she holds my most precious secret in her head, and that makes her far more dangerous than I ever thought she'd be.

"What about you?" she says, looking at me now.

I smile. "I'm always fine. Hail your cab."

The main raises his hand. "Hold on, she can't—"

I kick his Achilles tendon. "Here's how you know I'm telling the truth: I love this shirt and if I have to kill you, I'll get blood all over it. Do you know how hard blood is to wash off? I do. You can never get it off. Not ever." Never, never, never, never. Tap tap tap tap. "So you let her leave and I let you keep your blood on the inside where it belongs and we go talk to your friend who is so desperate to see me."

Pixie looks scared. "Fia, don't—"

"Get a cab. Now." I glare at her and she turns, walking stiffly to the edge of the sidewalk. Two men move to follow her.

"Tell them," I whisper in the ear of my man.

"Let her leave," he says, his voice tight.

Pixie looks back at me as a cab stops and she climbs in. I give her a thumbs-up with the hand I have wrapped around the front of my man. Then she is gone and that means she is safe, so I don't really care what happens now. I'll be fine.

I let go of the man and he jumps away, rubbing at his neck and calling me nasty names under his breath. I toss the bottle to the side with a tinkle of glass and smile cheerfully. "See? Easy! Who wants to take me to my earnest suitor?"

I follow a tall, broad-shouldered man with a gun's bulk

pushing out the edge of his sports jacket. We walk around the corner to where a car idles in an alley. "Disappointing," I mutter. "I was hoping for a party bus."

He opens the back door to the car and gestures for me to go in. As I slip past him my hand darts to his belt and I snatch the gun, then yank the door shut and hit the lock.

"So!" I turn and point the gun at the man sitting next to me. "Surprise!"

A smile slides over his face like oil pooling on water and I wasn't ready for this, because I'm back—I'm back—oh no I don't want to remember what he makes me remember. Lips and hands and a dance floor and—

"Hello, Sofia," Rafael says.

I lean back against the plush leather seat and sigh, still training the gun on his head. "I didn't miss you." (His lips on mine, the first lips on mine, my first kiss, oh I want to be sick.)

He laughs, and his teeth are white and his throat is tan and I want to cut break cut smash it. I hate him. He is as slickly beautiful as ever, and I don't know what he's doing here but it's twisting my stomach and making the space behind my eyes heavy with the insistent pressure of wrong.

"How do you like New York?" he asks.

"If you brought me here for small talk, you could have used fewer guns. Just a thought."

"I was actually hoping you could help me with something.

See, I had a bit of a disappointment today. Something I've been working on for a while fell through."

The would-be assassin. "Whoops." I flash him an off-kilter grin, but inside the spinning needle whirls faster. I cannot believe I stopped her. I cannot believe it was right. I hate Rafael, hate his smell and the feel of him near me.

But maybe Rafael is the only person doing the right thing.

My stomach drops as I realize . . . oh, no.

Oh, no.

Lerner. Casey was working for Lerner.

She was working for *Rafael.*

Rafael is with Lerner.

Maybe not. Maybe she was so good she could think about Lerner to frame them. It's not right, I know it's not right, but I cling to it. She didn't think about Rafael, she didn't!

He smiles and everything buzzes, feels off, more off than ever before. "You win some, you lose some. And when I heard you were finally in deep with Daddy Keane, well, that changed everything. Let's talk about how you're going to help me."

"Why would I help you?" I whisper.

"James was."

"Liar," I snarl.

"I didn't tell him about Casey. Shame, really. You would have liked her. She was my fail-safe, put into action because James broke his promises. We were supposed to build our own army together—him on the inside, me on the outside. Take down his father. Lately, however, I think he likes being daddy's pet more than he wants revenge. Does that feel familiar to you, Fia? Promises strung out along months, tentative ideas for a future that never seems to get here, no matter how close you keep getting?" He leans forward intently.

No. No no no. James wouldn't back out. Rafael is a liar. I can only trust James. If James is wrong, if James is lying to me, then I am wrong and if I am wrong, nothing is ever right again. If I cannot trust myself to love the right person, what can I trust?

Rafael can see that I'm wavering. He sits back, pulls out his phone as though he can't be bothered to pay full attention to the conversation. "We have another friend in common. Sweetest girl. She's like a sane version of you. Goes by Annie."

The world drops out from underneath me.

Annie.

There's a rather insistent-bordering-on-panicked tapping; Rafael opens the window and I realize the tapping this time wasn't in my head. I can't always tell.

The man who escorted me here is red-faced. "You okay, sir?"

Rafael waves a hand dismissively. "Relax. Sofia and I are old friends. Isn't that right?"

Rafael's man has his arm through the window, trying to unlatch the door. I let him, then kick it open, slamming it into his stomach. I pull it back shut, then smash the gun against the side of Rafael's head.

"Annie is dead," I hiss. I hold the gun to his temple. There's a trickle of blood running down and the barrel disrupts its path. I wonder how the blood would have fallen if I didn't get in the way. I change things. All the time. I change them to be how I want them to be. "I killed her."

Rage is written into the lines of his mouth, but he peels his lips back into a smile. "Here." He holds out a card between two fingers. "My number. You'll call."

I take the card. His smile grows bigger. He knows he's won. I lower the gun and shoot the seat directly between his legs. He jumps, slamming himself into the corner of the seat, cursing me in fluid Italian. The scent of gunpowder assails my nose and I breathe in deeply, letting it settle in my sinuses.

I climb out of the car, pointing the gun at the men outside. "It's okay!" Rafael shouts, and they lower their guns. I turn and walk down the alley.

"You need me," Rafael yells after me. "You'll call. James betrayed us all. But you and I still want the same thing."

I throw the gun in a trash can, my fist clenched around his card. "I don't know what I want," I whisper, and it's true.

ANNIE

Six Weeks Before

~

I THROW A PUNCH. I MIGHT AS WELL THROW IT AWAY, because as usual it sails wildly through the air, connecting with nothing. "Do I look as stupid as I feel? Because I really can't imagine how that's possible."

Cole doesn't answer, but I hear a muffled laugh.

"Fia is the one who got trained to fight. For rather obvious reasons they didn't bother with me."

"I'm very familiar with how Fia fights."

I smirk. "I'm so glad one of us kicked your butt."

"I didn't say that." He sounds decidedly grumpy.

"Didn't have to. Fia's got perfect instincts. Never hesitates. Operates on pure impulse. Blah, blah, blah." I throw my arms in the air and then sit, defeated, on the floor next to the wall. If Fia were here, I wouldn't need to learn how to fight.

It was supposed to be the two of us, hiding, on the run. We would have made a good team. Wouldn't we? Or would she have felt like she used to feel, like she had to take care of me all the time? Maybe if she were around, I wouldn't mind. I let people take care of me as a default.

I'm sick of it.

My thoughts drift to the bottle of pills buried in the bottom of my bag upstairs. I still haven't started taking them. I wanted to ask Sarah what it was like, if it helped, but she and Rafael left as soon as we got to this tiny house in Tennessee. They said it was to muddy the trail, and they'll meet back up with us when they feel like it's safer. So I'm stuck here with only Cole.

A foot nudges my shoulder, hard, and I twist and shove it away. Cole? Not such pleasant company.

"You have strengths, too. Good balance," he says. "And you recognized the Keane employee's voice after years."

I stand, trying not to groan. "It's not like I have superhearing or some sort of bat sense. No mystical blind-person powers."

His voice is dry. "Other than the whole seeing-the-future thing."

I flip him off.

"Put your hand on my shoulder. Notice anything?"

I frown. I do, actually. His shoulder is covered with muscle. My shoulders do *not* feel like that. "Umm, it's very . . . shouldery?"

He shoves lightly against my hand. "Think of the angle."

It takes me a few more seconds, then I laugh. "You're short!"

"We're about the same height, which puts you at five foot six. Average for a girl. Small for a guy."

"So you use this to your advantage?"

"Nobody suspects the little ones. I also have a very charming smile."

I snort. "Doubtful. Does anyone ever even see it?"

"Sometimes. Now. You're going to be best in close quarters. Let's work on judo techniques. Fast and dirty throws, maximum pain, and then you run."

"Okay. I'm ready. What do I do?"

"Stand there and look defenseless."

I kick at his shin, but miss. As usual. So I opt to stick my tongue out, and then I stand still and look defenseless. It's easy.

He grabs me from behind, locking his hands around my waist and pinning my arms at my side. I've never noticed how he smells before. It's soft, barely a trace, but he smells like . . . soap. It's a clean, honest scent, not advertising anything but the truth.

"Help, help," I say, raising my voice an octave. "I am so defenseless. Woe is me."

"What do you have free?"

My feet, my head. Without stopping to think about the consequences, I slam my head back into his face.

He lets go, swearing and stomping.

"Oh my gosh, I'm so sorry." I turn around, hands over my mouth in horror. "I didn't mean to! I should have warned you! Or said what I should do instead of actually doing it. Did I break your nose? Are you bleeding?"

His voice is strained and muffled, but I think it's amused. I hope it's amused. "No, that was good. Noses are always good. Groins, too. If you can find his legs, you can hit his groin."

I feel myself blushing, but I nod. "Done?"

"No, not done. I'm going to grab you and you're going to get away. However you need to."

He doesn't wait for me to agree.

Ten minutes later we're both panting. He has me by the hair; I grab at his hand.

"Ignore it," he says. "You can afford to lose hair. Focus on getting away."

I slam my elbow back, hitting his ribs, then twist under his hand, my hair ripping at my scalp and making my eyes tear. I bring my knee up to hit him in the stomach, but I miss.

"Good! Really good!"

"What are you doing?" Adam sounds horrified. Cole and I freeze, his hand still wrapped up in my hair, my hands around his other wrist. I was about to bite him.

Oh kill me. Why would Adam show up *now*?

Cole disentangles his hand, and his voice comes out far calmer than mine would. "We're practicing."

"Practicing *what*? Annie, you're crying, are you okay? What did he do?" Adam's arm comes around my shoulders, and I hurriedly wipe under my eyes.

"No, I'm not crying, my eyes are watering. From the hair. It's okay. I'm learning self-defense."

"She's not going to get in any fights!"

Cole's voice is the verbal equivalent of a shrug. "Better to know."

"She doesn't need to know! What is wrong with you? She's *blind*!"

His words whip across my face and my spine stiffens. I know I'm blind, obviously, but hearing him put it like that, the way someone would say *She's a child!* wriggles under my skin.

"She's not your responsibility," Cole says.

"She is! Fia gave *me* the number to call. Fia trusted *me* with the most important person in her whole life. I'm not going to let anything happen to Annie! You *shot* Fia. You don't care about what she would want."

"Why should I? Fia's not here."

"But she will be."

I back away from their voices, then raise my hand. "Umm, hey. Can I have an opinion on this?" I turn toward Adam. Is this how he sees me? I want to pretend like he's protecting me because I'm precious, not because he thinks I'm defective. "I've spent most of my life feeling helpless. Being *made* to feel helpless. I'm done feeling like that."

"But you'll never need to know this stuff," Adam says, and he sounds so sad I forgive him.

I walk forward and hold my arms out, wait for him to meet me, and then put my arm around his waist. "None of us wants to be part of this, but we're all here. Besides, it's kind of fun. And now I can do this. Look! Over in the corner!" I point wildly, then put my foot behind Adam's leg and throw my shoulder against his stomach, tripping him. I fall on top of him, then roll off, laughing. "See how good I'm getting?"

"Brilliant," Cole says, his voice dark.

Adam lets out a winded *oof*.

I sit up, still laughing, gasping for breath between giggles.

"Come on. We have another half hour to go." Cole nudges me with his foot, and I grab his ankle, holding on for dear life as he tries to get loose. "Seriously, Annie, we're not done."

I lunge forward and wrap my arms around his knees, push against them until he loses his balance and crashes to the ground.

"I win!" I cackle, flopping onto my back.

It'd feel more like a victory if Adam's voice saying "She's blind!" wasn't echoing in my head, making me feel small and helpless.

His words are still there that afternoon as I sit alone in my room while Cole and Adam talk business. I miss Fia so much it's like I've lost another sense, one I didn't know I had until it was gone.

She would know what to do. She would tell me.

And that's exactly my problem. I've had enough of waiting for other people. I tap out two pills and swallow them, then lie back on my bed and wait.

After a couple of hours someone knocks softly on my door. "Come in," I call. I feel weird. But not super weird. And maybe I only feel weird because I'm waiting to feel weird. I don't know.

"Hey," Adam says. "It's been a while. How are things?"

I laugh. "You know, same old, same old. Attacked by people from my past with guns. Ran from their bodies. Got stuck in this house to hide some more. You?"

I feel him sit on the edge of the bed. "It's been okay. Having a lab again makes me feel a little normal. Been running tests on Sarah and a few other girls. Actually, that's why I'm here. Rafael wanted me to get some scans of your brain activity."

I sit up, frowning. "You're researching?"

"Pretty much picking up where I left off, but it's nice because I'm not operating blind anymore. Err. I know what I'm looking at, now, I mean."

"Be careful. I—you could do a lot of damage." I bite my lip, hesitating. Nope. No more hedging. "I knew about you before we met."

"What did Fia tell you?" He sounds so bashfully pleased with the thought that Fia talked about him, it makes what I'm saying feel even worse.

"Actually, I knew about you first. From a vision. It was

women, a bunch of women, who could Read and See and Feel. They were coming into focus and then disappearing. It wasn't a happy vision. It was a bad one. And your name was there the whole time."

"Annie, I would never hurt anyone." He's upset, and he stands up from the bed, starts pacing. "You have to believe that."

"Of course I believe that! But right now it's so hit-and-miss finding girls like me. If someone, the wrong someone, got hold of what you're doing, if they could track abilities on a broad scale, none of these girls would be safe."

"I know. We'll be careful. I'd die before I let Keane get my research. I understand if you don't want to—"

He pauses, and then I hear the distinct rattle of a medicine bottle being picked up. "What's this?"

"A prescription. I wanted to see if it'd help me have more visions."

"Adderall?"

"It increases brain function."

"I know what it is. It's essentially legalized speed. How long have you been taking it?"

"Just today." I frown. He's annoying me. I don't want to talk about this. I want to go for a walk. I should go for a walk. I stand and try to leave, but he grabs my arm.

"Wait. I've seen visions happening on an MRI with Sarah. They're seizures. Or at least they act almost the same way. And

I'm pretty sure this type of medicine can trigger seizures if you're already prone to them."

"Or trigger visions."

"Let me look up the side effects, okay? I wish you had talked to me before taking them."

"I took them a couple hours ago. Obviously nothing is happening." I jerk my arm away and walk out of my room. I don't know this house well yet, and I miss the top stair, almost falling.

"Whoa," Cole says, catching me around the waist. "What's going on?"

"Going for a walk! Or a run. I haven't ever been for a run."

Adam talks behind me. "She took something."

Another rattle as the bottle is tossed from Adam to Cole. Cole swears loudly. "Did Rafael give these to you?"

"I asked for them."

"I'm going to kill him. Get Sarah on the phone right now."

I open my mouth to argue but it's hot, it's so hot in here, and I feel like I'm already running, like the world is spinning under my feet faster than it used to, and then there is light

so much light

and it comes at me and comes at me and doesn't stop

FIA

Twenty-eight Hours Before

~

I WAKE UP TREMBLING AND CRYING. I KILLED THEM. I killed them again. I always kill them.

James's arms come around me, hold me close, hold me together. He holds me together.

If it weren't for his arms, I don't know what I'd do.

"Nobody actually lives in North Dakota," I say, drinking coffee even though it's early enough I should go back to bed. I'm sitting on the floor next to the couch. Hotel furniture is creepy.

I texted Pixie that I was safe, but fell asleep waiting for James to get back. I don't want to fall asleep again, not if James is leaving.

I can't think about Rafael, about what I found out tonight.

Or I can. I forget that thoughts are safe around James. Thoughts never feel safe anymore. But—oh, what did I do? What did I do, giving Annie to Lerner?

"Have you ever met someone from North Dakota?" I ask, trying to distract myself.

James laughs, neatly folding a pair of slacks before setting them in his luggage. "No, I haven't."

"No one has. That's because it's not a real place."

"I'll be gone two days, tops."

I stand and run my fingers along his clothes, each placed perfectly in the luggage. "Why do you have to go?"

"Because, pet, it's important."

I pick up his slacks, wrinkle them into a ball, and shove them back in. "I'm *not* your pet."

"Fia." He puts his arms around my waist, pulls me close, kisses my forehead with his lips pulled back into a smile. "You don't get it. He trusts me. He trusts *you*. This is it. Any hesitation he had about us is gone after what you did. Just play it safe and do whatever anyone tells you to. And if anyone asks, you don't know where I am and you're annoyed because I never tell you enough about what's going on."

"Gee, that will be hard to fake." I glare at him, and he looks hurt. He does it to protect me—in case things go wrong, in case he messes up, he hopes maybe I'll get out okay. But sometimes I wonder, if he spends all his time at work thinking that he doesn't really care about me, that I'm just a tool he's crafted . . .

How many lies can a brain tell itself before they become truths?

I soften my look and his shoulders relax from the tension nearly always written there. "We're close," he says. "Closer than we've ever been."

Close. Closer. Rafael's words bounce around in my skull, making my head hurt. I hate that he has space in my skull now. I don't believe him about James—I *don't*—but I can't stop thinking it. Does Rafael have Annie, or does he just know she's alive? If he's Lerner, and Lerner are the good guys, is Rafael a good guy?

No.

James is my good. "Tell me," I say. "Tell me what we're going to do. Tell me what getting closer to your father has brought us. I want a timeline."

He strokes my back. "Remember our deal? We don't talk about it. We don't think about it. We don't plan it."

"Of course I remember," I snarl. I have been not thinking and not planning and not not not not for so long I don't know if I could think and plan anymore if my life depended on it.

"It's important." The line appears between his eyebrows, and I smooth it away with my thumb. He is so beautiful, this fierce, manipulative, calculating boy of mine. He is a liar. I chose him, I love him, I couldn't love him if it wasn't right. He takes care of me. He saves me from myself.

"Have you ditched the Reader yet?"

I shrug, dropping my hand. I thought about killing her tonight. I saved her, instead. "I like her."

"You can't afford to like her. What if you thought the wrong thing? What if you thought about Annie?"

I rub my own forehead, tap tap tap tap against it. "I am so sick of hearing about Annie."

"Where else did you hear about her?" His voice is sharp and tight with suspicion. He does not suspect enough. Never enough about me.

I should tell him about Rafael. If I trusted him, I would ask him about Rafael. I would bring him in on this problem, and I would let him help me fix it. Instead I smile. "In my head, all the time, I have to sing the *I killed Annie* song. It's a very repetitive tune."

Sometimes I forget it's not true. Sometimes, like tonight, I wake up and see the blood on her hand, and I can't remember whether or not I actually killed her. It scares me more than anything.

Maybe I did kill her.

No. I know I didn't. I saved her. I killed for her.

"Do you have any way of contacting her?"

"Nope." Annie is *mine.* My secret. My sister. Mine. I add this to the secrets I keep from James. I don't even know why I keep the ones I do, why I hide the things I do. I can't stop.

He slams his suitcase shut, zips it up. "Did you really have to leave her with Lerner?"

I roll my eyes. "The foster care system denied my application." It was right to leave her there. I know it was. I remember what it felt like. I have to trust that, or I'll lose my mind.

Well, lose it more.

He picks up his bag and leans in to kiss me, but I turn my face away. "Did I do the right thing?" I whisper.

He drops the bag, pulls me into his arms, tries to get me to look at him. "You always do. Which thing are we talking about?"

I am talking about so many things. So many things. I look him in the eyes, try to see myself reflected back, but I can't. There's nothing there. "Your father would have died. I stopped it."

The lines around his eyes tighten, and without moving he's gotten farther away from me.

"Doesn't he deserve to die?" I ask.

He closes his eyes and then leans his head against mine. "I don't know, Fia. When I realized what would have happened, I . . . was relieved. I was glad he wasn't dead. Maybe I should want him dead, but I don't. I want to destroy him, I want him ruined and behind bars, but I can't want him dead. He's all I have left."

I drop my hands as his words echo through me. He looks up, a heartbeat too late, and shakes his head. "No, no, I didn't mean that. I mean he's all the family I have left. Like Annie. Would it matter to you if Annie did the worst thing in the world, if she took away everything you loved, if she was a terrible person? Would you want her dead?"

"No." The word drops from my lips, but it has no soul, no passion behind it. Do I want Phillip Keane dead? Would I ever do that to James?

Well, obviously not. I saved the monster's life. "What happens to the woman?" I ask.

James clears his throat, checks his pockets for his keys or his cell phone. I know before he opens his mouth he will lie to me. "I'm not sure."

My brain is exploding with all the wrongs clashing against each other—she'll die, or she's dead, or she's been dead for months, she just didn't know it yet. And it's my fault. I traded Phillip Keane's life for hers.

But then James kisses me and his lips are soft and warm and they push it away, they push everything away, as always.

We are both of us made of the things we have lost. I want to find those things together. "Tell me about your mother," I whisper.

He freezes against me, then with a sigh that travels through his whole body, he sits on the couch, pulling me onto his lap.

"She told the worst jokes in the world. She loved a good pun."

"No such thing."

His smile is the saddest I've ever seen. "She was a terrible cook. Burned everything."

"Did she love your father?" How could a woman who could see the future—who could know what was coming—fall in love with a man like Phillip Keane?

James leans his head back, closes his eyes. There is something painfully innocent about the curve of his thick, dark lashes against his face. "She told me only people we love the most can destroy us, because no one else has that kind of power."

"So she knew."

He nods. "She knew. Do you know what else she always said?" He's quiet and still for so long I wonder if he's fallen asleep. Then, his voice barely above a whisper, he says, "She'd hold me close and say, 'James, my darling boy, you are going to break my heart.' And I'd promise I wouldn't, and she'd look at me and I could see in her face that she knew. She *knew* I would. And when I got older, it made me so mad that I did exactly what she said. She gave me the same power she gave my father, and we destroyed her."

I bury my face in the space between his neck and shoulder, breathe him in, wish my cursed instincts could tell me what to say to him, how to pull him back to me. "It wasn't your fault."

"Nothing ever is." His laugh rattles something broken free in his chest, a bitter exhalation of weight that I cannot carry for him.

If we are defined by what we have lost, James and I will never really be found.

* * *

I wink at the security guard, then put on my best bored mood for the Feeler in the corner of the room. She's here to monitor me while I do stock-picking duties. Can't feel anything I want to feel. Not about James, not about Rafael, not about Annie. What else is new.

I'm three floors beneath Pixie. Three floors beneath Phillip Keane.

Humming to myself, I sit down at a desk and flip through the Dow and NASDAQ. I pick at random, whatever strikes my fancy. Sell this. Buy that. Tra-la-la-la. They are all imaginary numbers anyway. They don't give me account information and computers here, not like James gives me. So I can't change things, can't hide things. Oh well.

I finish, stretching my arms above my head and yawning. Saved the boss's life yesterday. What to do today? Maybe I'll rescue a deposed Middle Eastern dictator. Who knows what my instincts will decide is right!

The Feeler sets a stack of folders on my desk, watching me way too intently. "More stocks?" I ask. I am not curious, but I don't need to feel curious for this. I still feel bored. And hungry. "Can empaths feel when I'm hungry?"

She doesn't look amused. Maybe because her hair is pulled back into a ponytail so tight, the corners of her hazel eyes are tugged out. I'm glad I can't feel what her scalp must feel like.

Feelers have the worst skills of all.

Or maybe Pixie does. I don't want to know what everyone thinks of me.

Or maybe James's mom did. If the people I love are going to destroy me, at least I don't have to live with it every day until it happens.

The Feeler snaps her fingers in front of my face. My eyes meet hers and I don't bother hiding the violent feelings that flare up. "Mr. Keane wants you to go over these old notes. You aren't the only one working on them." She says that last like a threat and I'm confused by her hostility. And then I wonder.

"You didn't happen to know Clarice, did you?"

Her eyes narrow.

"Ah, okay. Well, sorry about that. But look!" I raise both hands in the air and smile at her. "No chairs!"

I tap tap tap tap my foot on the floor. Calm. I am calm. I am calm and bored. I am the ocean. I am the yacht in the middle of the ocean. I am nothing.

I am flames.

Not yet. Not yet.

"Get to work," she snarls.

The first sheet is handwritten, dated almost three years ago. Something about the writing feels familiar.

"What is this?" I ask, trying to buy time, needing to calm myself down. The ocean. The ocean. The ocean. Nothing.

"We found them cleaning out storage bins at the school." The Feeler smiles, and I am glad I can't feel what she is feeling right now. "Clarice's notes on visions she had for potential students. A bit of a treasure trove."

I let a giddy burst of something twisted flare up as I laugh, my smile broken glass. "Awesome. How great. Clarice comes back from the dead to help us out! That's just like her. She was always so thoughtful."

I tap tap tap tap, tap tap tap tap, tap tap tap tap on the paper. James says it's okay to give them reactions they expect. It'd be okay for me to feel disturbed, or guilty, or sad about this reminder of Clarice.

If I start that, I can never, ever stop.

So instead I wash it all away and just read. Most of it is incomprehensible. I scowl, flipping through pages describing locations and people without names. "Seers are useless," I mutter, tossing away a page describing, at length, a woman's color of nail polish as she waves good-bye from the back of an unidentifiable bus.

I blink, eyes frozen to the next page and the name on it.

Sadie.

"I thought we wrote off Sadie as lost after what happened in Des Moines?" I say as casually as I can manage. It's okay to feel anxious about that name. There's a lot of baggage. I can feel a little anxious.

I can still hear Clarice, the way her mouth twisted into a smile around Sadie's name as she recommended that I do something to make sure the girl's family wouldn't come looking for her. I can still remember how in control I felt as I said no, how sure I was that they could never make me do anything like that again.

I can still remember what it felt like to go out a month ago to bring Sadie in, making Clarice's death even more pointless. I can still remember the blood on my hands from that trip. The look on Annie's face. *No.* Annie is dead. The look on Eden's face, horrified, judging me.

I hated Eden.

"Turn the page. There are additions. We've got a new location that a Seer found yesterday." The Feeler is staring intently at me, feeling everything I feel. I am sad. I am tired. I am lost. This is all wrong, every bit of it, everything. I am wrong.

I am not any of those things. I am fine. They found Sadie again. I am excited. See how excited I am? "Let's bring her in."

ANNIE

Six Weeks Before

~

A GIRL, TWIRLING IN A DRESS, THE LIGHT SPINNING around her as she laughs. She stops, staggers to the side, dazed.

Then she's older, and Fia is walking with her down a hall, talking and smiling and nodding.

The hall they're in is at the school.

Another girl, hair in hundreds of intricate braids, sitting next to a crashed bike, crying. But she isn't hurt, her friend is, skinned knees raw and bleeding. The girl with the braids keeps crying.

Then she's older, and Fia is sitting in a small room on a couch across from her and an older man, nodding and smiling and drinking tea. Fia's wearing a dress jacket and a skirt, and she looks false, she looks so false I want to scream, want to tell them that it's a lie. This Fia is a lie.

Another girl, dressed all in black, hands pulled into her sleeves, sitting curled in a ball in the corner of the couch. An older woman who looks tired and drawn signs a paper, her eyes devoid of hope. James and Eden, older than she was when I saw her in a vision years ago, watch. Fia leans against the wall, staring out the window, then turns and smiles at the girl. She taps on her leg, tap tap taps, but no one notices. "You're going to love the school," Fia says. There is something wary and terrified in Fia's eyes.

Another girl, tiny, barely to Fia's shoulder, looking at her with hope and desperation. Fia smiles, but there's no life in her face. "It'll get better now, Amanda," she says. James pats the girl on the head. "She's going to love it there, Ms. Lafayette," he says. A woman hugs the girl, crying, and the girl starts crying, too, looking at Fia like Fia can make it stop. Fia nods.

And then another girl.

Another girl.

Another girl.

Another girl.

So many girls.

Girl after girl after girl, following Fia, because Fia instantly understands what to say, what to feel, how to act to get them to want to come. She's leading them to the school, and they want it, and she *knows*. She knows what she's doing.

I want to scream but I can't. I can do nothing but watch. I

watch and watch until the colors and lights bleed into one constant swirl I can no longer understand, and I miss the darkness but the light won't stop.

"Annie? I think she's waking up."

I open my eyes and I'm so relieved to see nothing, I burst into tears.

"What happened?" I ask, trying to sit up, but my muscles tremble and shake, and I feel like I haven't eaten in three days. I'm dizzy and light-headed and everything hurts. I'm going to throw up. "Bathroom," I gasp, putting my hands over my mouth.

Someone picks me up and runs, then sets me down on a tile floor and I hug the toilet like it can save me.

My hair is pulled back gently from my face and held at the base of my neck. A cold sweat has broken out on my body and I'm still shaking, but the nausea passes and I think I'll be okay.

I try to stand and that's when my stomach decides it is not okay. Vomiting until there's nothing left, my stomach muscles cramped with spasms, I finally lean to the side, hitting the bathtub and sitting against it.

"Here," Cole says, handing me a washcloth, damp with cool water. I wipe my mouth, too wrung out and hollowed to be embarrassed that it was him holding my hair back while I puked. He takes the washcloth and then hands me a small towel, also cool and damp, and I put it against my forehead, wipe the back of my neck, rest my cheek on it.

The last time someone held my hair for me while I puked, I had the stomach flu and Eden stayed with me. I know my old life was a lie, but it was a nice lie, and I miss the ease of false security.

"You had a seizure," he says, sitting next to me.

I take a deep breath, even my lungs sore. "How long did it last?"

"Ten minutes," Adam says, taking my wrist to feel my pulse. "That's bad, Annie. You're hitting oxygen deprivation danger if it goes much longer than that. Brain damage."

"I was only out for ten minutes?"

"No," Cole says. "You've been asleep for almost four hours. You didn't wake up after the seizure ended. We were about to take you to the hospital."

"Can't go to the hospital. We don't have the right documents. I'll be okay."

"Why would you risk that?" Cole's voice is hard, and I flinch, turning my head away from him. "What could possibly be worth risking your life for?"

"I didn't know it was so risky."

"Because you didn't ask us about it! I could have told you what it did to Sarah! I can't believe Rafael gave you the drugs."

"Did she have seizures, too?"

"No. But she hasn't been sleeping. She barely eats. Isn't it enough that you two have these visions take over and intrude on your brains, without forcing your bodies to do more?"

I lean my head on the bathtub. The rounded edge fits against my skull and I feel like I could fall asleep here. "It worked," I whisper.

"No, it didn't."

"It did. I saw her. Fia. Over and over again. With girls. She's—" I swallow hard, reminding myself that there's nothing left in my stomach to lose. "She's finding girls for the school. She's recruiting."

"How can you trust what you saw? You were on drugs."

I shake my head, back and forth along the bath, then let it drift and rest against Cole's shoulder. "Maybe. You're right. You have to be right. She wouldn't do that. Why would she do that?"

He doesn't answer.

"Think," Sarah says, her voice over the phone soft but insistent. She sounds exhausted. I want to ask if she's been able to sleep yet, if she's gone off the Adderall. What she's seen. "Details. We need details. Names, locations, anything that sticks out enough for us to be able to find these girls. We only need one to confirm whether or not what you saw was real."

I squeeze my eyes shut, my head throbbing. This headache has lasted for two days now, and I think I'll go mad if it doesn't stop soon. "Amanda. Fia called one of the girls Amanda. And

James said . . ." I play it over in my head, trying to isolate that single thread, but there are so many, so many faces and scenes and images. "Ms. Lafayette! He called her mom Ms. Lafayette."

"Okay. You keep thinking and pulling out any more details you can. Rafael and I will find Amanda, if she exists."

"But it worked for you, didn't it? The pills. You've been seeing more."

There's a long pause, and when Sarah finally answers, she sounds haunted. "Yes. I've been seeing more."

"So it works."

Her laugh is bitter and harsh and nothing like the Sarah I've known. "Yeah, it works. I'll call you when we know something."

She hangs up, and I sit, holding the phone in my hand, hoping against hope that there is no Amanda Lafayette in the world. Please, please let her not be real.

Let it not be real.

FIA

Nineteen Hours Before

~

"WE'RE LIKE THE WORST COMIC BOOK EVER," PIXIE says, scowling behind massive round sunglasses. Palm trees reflect from their lenses, the Tampa sunshine brutal and heavy. We're sitting outside a café, though anyone with a brain would be inside with air-conditioning. Not us. We have to watch for a teenage girl whose life needs ruining.

Again.

"The Adventures of Sullen and Psycho. It has a nice ring to it." I bounce my legs, buzz buzz buzz buzzing with energy. Not the good kind. The kind that warns I am too close to the edge, too far down the slope, in danger of sliding off and away and being lost forever. Oh, this is wrong, this is all wrong, everything is wrong so wrong.

"We should leave, then," Pixie whispers.

I imagine invisible fishing lines, hooking the corners of my mouth and tearing at the skin there, pulling my lips back into a simulation of a smile. The same threads connected to my arms and legs, jerking me like a gangly marionette. Go here. Do this. Smile. Ignore the wrong. Make it work. Make it work.

"No, we have to do this." They put me on a private plane with Pixie as soon as I said Sadie was viable. Sadie, Sadie, slipped through the cracks in the aftermath of Clarice's murder. (Ha ha ha ha, tap tap tap tap, Clarice's murder, I can think that like it was an episode on *Law and Order*, something that sometimes airs on cable channels and you think "Oh, I remember that, it was the innocent-looking teenager" right before you switch to something else, something safe, but nothing is safe not ever safe nothing is ever safe.) Then we found Sadie and then we lost her and now we've found her again.

Sadie. I hate her. I have never even seen her and because of her I am twice steeped in blood, like one of Annie's teas, a rich dark red steaming into my face, bathing me in blood, always blood, and I can't stop holding the cup, and—

"Fia," Pixie says, her mouth twisted up. "*What* is your brain doing right now?"

Backtrack the thoughts. Slipped through the cracks. Sadie slipped through the cracks twice. But no one can avoid fate. I am fate. I am the pale, horrible hands of fate, and now I've come for Sadie again, and it's wrong to be here but it's wrong to be everywhere, so here is fine.

Pixie rubs her temples. *Am I giving you a headache?* I think.

"You *are* a headache."

I grin. Lean back in my chair. It's okay. This is fine. Just one more step, one more thing to do, I can turn it off, turn it all off. This has to be done. I think about James, instead, think about his lips to drown out the constant ringing of wrong in my ears, to reset my equilibrium. James said to do whatever they asked me to. I love James.

I love him.

We'll make everything right.

Pixie mimes vomiting into the planter next to our table. "Please go back to the crazy-train thoughts. I can't stomach hearing someone think about him that way."

"Jealous."

"Yes, please, someone get me my own sociopathic, sex-obsessed slimeball! How can I go on without a man like that in my life?"

"You don't know him," I snap, surprised by how much her criticism of him stings. Is it because we're friends now? I think Pixie is my only friend in the whole world besides James. And I've known her all of two days? Three? I don't know her. And she's dangerous, I keep forgetting.

I drain the rest of my smoothie, then look at her. "The last time I came to find Sadie, a girl ended up dead." Tap tap tap TAP. I hate that TAP. I hate it I hate it so much so much.

Her shoulders sink, and she leans over to me, nudging my arm. "I know about Eden. They told me. I'm sorry, Fia."

She smiles, but the smile is a lie, a preamble to what is coming next. The ice in my stomach from the smoothie spreads outward and I don't want to hear her anymore.

"Have you ever asked James about his . . . particular life ambitions?" Her voice is as casual as a knife in the gut.

I scowl, tug on my boot top, and wish I'd worn sandals. "What ambitions would a sociopathic sex-obsessed slimeball possibly need?"

"He's got a lot of plans," she says, watching me closely. "I care about you, Fia, and I'm not trying to drive you away from him. I don't understand it, but I know you need him. I've seen your thoughts when you've been away from him for too long. But you have to have your eyes open. You have to have enough information to make decisions."

I throw my cup. It sails through the air and lands in the trash can without touching the sides. "I never need information to make decisions. There's Sadie." Now we have something to do and I can stop thinking and start doing.

It's strange, finally seeing her as more than a photo. I never actually saw her in Iowa. My heart flutters. Maybe this is what it's like to see a movie star in real life, this strange slowing and stopping of time, the recognition of knowing someone you don't actually know. Sadie's done so much to my life for never having been in it.

Her long hair is pulled into a ponytail at the base of her neck. She's aggressively plain—no makeup, clothes dark and baggy. In spite of the weather she's wearing a collared shirt, buttoned all the way up, and over that a hoodie jacket, with her hands shoved into the pockets. She trudges by, purse slung across her body. Her shoulders are turned in, her eyes on the ground.

Everything about her pleads to be ignored. I'm so sorry, Sadie.

"What do you know about her?" Pixie asks.

"Seer. She's been flagged before, but she was nabbed by Lerner and we lost her. Either she's broken with Lerner or they screwed up, because someone picked up her trail again yesterday. And here we are."

"She doesn't want to come with us, then."

"It's not really up to her." One way or another, Sadie is going to the school.

I slide unnoticed onto the sidewalk behind her and watch as she navigates the space. There's an almost dance to the way she twists and turns to avoid other people, the intense focus it must take to remain untouched moving through a crowd.

Pixie swears. "You're right. She's thinking, 'Don't touch me, don't touch me, don't touch me.' It's like being in *your* head—she's adamant, obsessive about it. I doubt if she even knows she's thinking it, but she's not thinking anything else. Just that, over and over again."

We keep following, watching her move with a runner's grace belied by her horrible posture.

Pixie shakes her head, piercings glinting in the sun as she raises an eyebrow. "Maybe she was . . . maybe someone . . . *hurt* her. In a . . . way." Pixie looks at me helplessly.

It isn't that simple. Not that there would be anything simple about a situation like that, but it would be its own tragedy. Not one that would have put her in Keane's Seers' line of sight so many times. "We need to touch her, see what happens."

That's the key, I know it is, because when I think about touching her, everything in me screams to stop, to stay away, to avoid doing exactly that. I can listen to the directions of wrong as well as right. Pick the one thing you shouldn't do, and do it. That's how I became a model employee. That's how I filled the school with the most promising new students they've ever had.

Maybe that's what went wrong when I saved Phillip Keane's life.

"So, what, run up and bump into her?" Pixie asks.

I narrow my eyes, take in all of Sadie. We don't know where she's staying. All we knew was that she'd walk by this café in the afternoon. Stupid Seers. But the strip malls have turned into residential streets, so we must be getting close.

"I don't think that'd work. Look at the way she's dressed—maximum skin coverage."

"Oh, so just run up to her and casually stroke her cheek! No biggie, then." Pixie huffs, digging a twenty-dollar bill out of her pocket. "I have to do everything. Hey!"

Sadie doesn't turn around, and Pixie jogs to close the gap between them. "Hey, you dropped this."

Sadie barely looks up, keeps walking. "No, I didn't."

"Yeah, you dropped it back there. Here." Pixie holds it out, walking backward in front of Sadie, smiling.

Sadie shrugs, leaving her hands in her pockets. "Keep it." She turns to look over her shoulder, and our eyes meet.

The blood drains from her face. She looks terrified, and then she looks sad, and then she looks the type of bone-deep, soul-weary tired I see reflected back at me from mirrors. There's a swelling of something I didn't know I could feel for anyone other than Annie. Compassion. I want to help her. I want to protect her, not because I like her, like how it is with Pixie. I want to protect Sadie simply because she needs protecting. She nods at me, a sort of resigned gesture, and then turns and walks toward home.

I let Pixie come back to me. Her eyes are wide. "Well?" I ask.

"She looked at my hand and thought, 'No way I want to see what this girl's future is like.' But when she saw you—when she saw you, she thought, 'I'm dead. I thought I'd have more time.

Oh well.' Why would she think that, Fia?" Pixie looks at me imploringly, begging me to explain to her why a girl I'd never met would equate me with her own death.

"I don't know," I say, and I'm falling apart because *I don't know*. Anything.

What has she seen? What does she know?

What do I do?

ANNIE

Five Weeks Before

~

I CRINGE AS SOMETHING SMASHES AGAINST THE WALL. Shattering glass rains down onto the tile floor.

"Stop defending her!" Sarah screams. "Five for five! Five times I've tried to get to these girls, and five times Fia has already been there!"

"I don't understand why—"

"No! You don't! Because you keep trying to figure out why she'd do that, what her plan is, but the thing is, she doesn't have one! She never has! She's doing whatever James tells her, because she's in love with him. Do you have any idea how much more effective their recruitment has gotten since Fia ditched you and went back to them?"

"Sarah," Rafael says, his voice flat with warning. "You need to calm down."

"You see what I'm seeing and then tell me if you can calm down!"

"Why don't you go for a walk?"

"Why don't you go to hell!" She takes a few deep, unsteady breaths, and when she talks again, it's restrained. "I'm sorry. You're right. I need to . . . I'll be back in a while."

The front door slams.

"I'm sorry about that," Rafael says. "The last few weeks have been hard on her."

I lean against the counter glumly. "I understand." Ever since Sarah called confirming that Amanda was a real person—a twelve-year-old girl now whisked away to the Keane Foundation—I've been fighting the cold dread creeping in my bones. There's a reason. There has to be a reason Fia would do this. Sarah's wrong, I know she is. Fia wouldn't do this otherwise.

I wish I could talk to her, call her, let her explain. But another part of me is terrified that if I did talk to her, she wouldn't be able to explain anything, and I'd know once and for all that I was wrong about her.

I can't be wrong about her. She's my baby sister. She's not evil.

Rafael's hands come down on either side of my neck, thumbs rubbing slow circles in the muscles there. "You have a lot of tension," he says.

I laugh. "Can't imagine why." His fingers feel heavenly, though. I close my eyes and barely hold back a sigh. "How long are you two here for?" They got in this morning, but Rafael has been with Adam the whole time in the makeshift office. Adam didn't go back when he was supposed to a few days ago. Something about a more "peaceful environment" here, but I have a sneaking suspicion he stuck around to keep an eye on me.

Sarah came with Rafael. I was looking forward to spending time with her again, but . . . well.

"We're leaving. I won't risk being in the same place as you for long, not after what happened before. Though I would rather keep you with me."

He sounds like honey, thick and sweet and earthy. I know he's flirting with me, and I can't help but be pleased. Who knows, maybe I don't meet the guy from my visions until I'm fifty. What's wrong with a little flirtation?

Rafael's hands guide me around until I'm facing him. I can feel the lines of him, leaning in close, brushing against me. He pushes a strand of hair off my face, tracing his fingers down my cheek and lingering on my earlobe as he tucks the hair back.

And then, so suddenly I startle, his lips are against mine. I feel like time has slowed down, but not in a dreamy, romantic way. Though I've idly daydreamed kissing him a few times, I can't seem to figure this out. I wonder what I should be doing—whether I ought to move my lips, or use my tongue, what I ought to do with my hands—and then I realize that if I'm standing here with his lips against mine, wondering these things, I am probably not feeling the way a girl should during her first kiss.

That stupid, stupid vision has ruined me. I really won't be able to enjoy kissing someone for fun, not knowing there's another someone out there who will make me feel the way I do in that vision by something as simple as holding my hand.

Rafael's lips are soft and warm and perfectly pleasant, though, so when he pulls back after a few seconds I try to smile. I'm sure it looks more goofy than alluring, because that's how I feel. I wish that kiss had been more than just two lips connecting. I could use a little magic in my life right now.

He laughs, a silent, soft exhalation. "You Rosen sisters. So beautiful and strange. I wish I could collect a dozen of you."

I slap his shoulder. "That is not a compliment."

He strokes my cheek again, leaving his fingers a few seconds longer than strictly necessary as someone else comes into the room.

"Your car is here," Cole growls.

"Focus on your sister," Rafael says. "And call me as soon as you see anything else." His cologne lingers in his wake and I sit on a bar stool, bemused and unsure what to make of this development. If it even was a development. He's Italian. Maybe they kiss a lot. It wasn't terrible. It was nice. But I don't think I'll care if it never happens again with him.

Huh. Kind of anticlimactic for having waited nineteen years.

"Are you okay?" Cole asks.

"Hmm? Oh, I'm fine."

I can feel him pacing in front of me. "Are you and Rafael—"

"Did you see that?" My cheeks burn.

"I—no, I mean, it's none of my business, but—be careful, okay? You're too honest for him."

"I'm too honest? What does that mean?"

"You have no guile. Everything you feel is written on your face." He sits on a stool next to me, drumming his fingers on the counter. "Like smiling. People smile all the time when they don't mean it. If they're nervous, if they're lying, if they don't know how to react to something. You never smile unless you mean it."

"Your laugh is the same way." I bite my lip, embarrassed at having admitted I notice things about him. There's a line there that feels too weird to cross. "Besides, I wasn't aware my smile made me unqualified to date Rafael."

He lets out an exasperated breath. "That's not what I mean."

I elbow his side, flashing a smile that is apparently more honest than most. "I'm kidding. I'll be careful. We're not—I'm not dating him or anything." The silence between us now feels heavy, laden with the awkwardness of *Cole* giving me romantic advice. Subject change. "Did you see Sarah?"

"Yes."

"I'm worried about her."

"She should be here with us. I don't like it."

"I wish I could see something that would help us, help her." I scowl, kicking my toes against the floor in frustration. "Maybe if I took a lower dosage."

"That's a stupid idea."

"Don't call me stupid!"

"I didn't call you stupid, I called the idea stupid. Quit trying to mess up your brain. If you really want to see more, you should take better care of it, not worse."

"What would you know about it?"

"Apparently more than you or Sarah!" He paces back and forth in front of me, footsteps louder than normal. "This is all pointless."

"Look, obviously you're miserable, so why don't you leave? Find something more important to do than babysitting stupid, pathetic me!"

He stops. "Annie, that's not—"

"Don't pretend like that's not how you feel. I've heard you say as much. You wanted me gone from the beginning. That's fine. Whatever. Go with Sarah and Rafael and then you won't have to deal with me and my stupid ideas."

He puts a hand on my arm but I jerk it away, then leave the room. I lock my bedroom door behind me, so frustrated I don't know what to do with myself. Sarah hates me. Cole hates me. Rafael obviously likes me but I can't be with him, and I don't know if I'd want to even if I could. Not if it meant we'd be more than flirty colleagues.

An hour later there's a timid knock.

"What?"

"Can we come in?" Adam asks.

I unlock the door, but stand in the doorway with my arms crossed. "Well?"

"We have presents," Adam says with a smile in his voice.

"Tea isn't a present." Though it does smell nice.

"Not just tea. We also have a yoga mat, and ginkgo biloba, and a CD called *Soothing White Noise*."

"That was his idea," Cole says. "And you're going for long walks. And getting to bed at a decent hour."

"Look, when I said you were babysitting me, I didn't mean you should actually start. You know my parents are dead, right? Even when they were alive, they paid really crap rates for babysitters."

"You want more visions?" Cole asks. "We're going to help your brain, not damage it. Now drink your tea and put on your shoes. Three miles walking a day, minimum."

I take the tea and sip at it, mumbling, "Taking drugs was a lot simpler."

Only Adam laughs.

* * *

"You're breathing wrong," Adam says.

"Seriously? You're critiquing my breathing?"

"No! I mean, the lady on the video, she's doing it with her stomach, not her shoulders."

I roll my eyes, but try to do what he says. The last few days have yielded no visions, but I'll admit I have more energy. Cole's been avoiding me, sending Adam on all the walks. Adam tries to talk about Fia. It's not as "centering" as I think Cole thinks it ought to be.

I take a deep breath, then let it out, trying to clear my mind, to let all the stress and worry drain out of the hollow spaces between my bones. Fill the space with nothing, instead.

And then there's a girl.

She's tall and thin, baggy clothes covering every inch of skin, the hood of her gray sweatshirt pulled up over her head, with a few strands of brown hair escaping. She leans against a wall, eyes down, hands shoved in her pockets, as people—teenagers? in school? they have backpacks, but unlike her they're all in shorts and short sleeves—swirl around her. A broadcast crackles through the hall. "Good morning, Hoover High Terriers! Don't forget to buy your raffle tickets. Last day!"

As the crowd thins, a hand comes down on her shoulder and she jerks away as though burned. "Get to class, Sadie," a woman says, not unkindly.

"Yeah," the girl, Sadie, mutters. She walks away, shoulders hunched, and then—

A tired woman, frayed around the edges, looks over a stack of papers. "It's been hard," she says. "What with the criminal case against my husband—" She looks up, alarmed. "He's innocent. We have no idea how he got implicated in this embezzlement scheme."

James nods, all false sympathy.

"The lawyer fees are bleeding us dry. They've foreclosed on the house. When the school offered before, we thought it was best to keep her close to us. We tried to help her. I thought we could handle it, but she's failing out. I don't know what else to do. With everything going on, I can't—we can't—"

The front door opens and Sadie walks in, a heavy backpack dragging her shoulders down. She takes in the strangers with hooded eyes, then walks along the wall straight past everyone and out of the room.

Her mother's shoulders shake and an arm comes around them. Eden offers her a tissue, her own eyes tearing up. She looks up at James and glares accusingly. He doesn't react. Seeing her there breaks my heart a little. Because she doesn't know—she can't know that I'm alive. She has to think they let Fia kill me.

And she's still helping them. Oh, Eden.

James continues. "This is the best thing for her, Mrs. Kavadellis. We have the resources to help her. Sadie is going to have a new life."

The woman nods, wiping under her eyes.

There's a knock at the door and the woman calls, "Come in."

Fia walks in, dressed in the school uniform, looking young and sweet except for the tension in her eyes.

"Oh, here's Sofia." James smiles paternally at her. "She's the girl I was telling you about. She was in Des Moines visiting relatives and so we thought she could stop by, talk with Sadie, answer any questions she has. It'll be easier if Sadie has a familiar face at the school."

"Sadie, can you come in here?"

Hands pulled into her sleeves, Sadie slouches in, immediately curling into a ball in the corner of the couch. Her mom signs the papers. James and Eden watch. Fia leans against the wall, staring out the window, then turns. Horror flashes across my sister's face. Eden looks up sharply, but Fia smiles brightly, falsely, at the girl. She taps on her leg, tap tap taps, but no one notices. "You're going to love the school," Fia says.

Then the darkness is back. ". . . asleep?"

I shudder, the pain dull and familiar behind my eyes. "Get Cole. I need to go to Iowa. Right now."

FIA

Eighteen Hours Before

WE SIT ON THE CURB A FEW LOTS DOWN FROM THE house where Sadie is staying. Pixie stretches her skinny legs out into the street. Good thing she's so short she's safe from having them run over.

She kicks at my boot. "Are the short jokes funny in your head? Because they aren't funny in mine."

"Shut it, Shortie." I dial James and wait for him to pick up. I am spinning out of control, I know I am, everything is spinning out of control and I don't know if I can do enough to hold on to everything, to twist everything in the way I do, but I have to try I will try.

I thought New York would change things, make me even more focused, put me directly in line with our goals. But I feel further away than ever from my flames, my beautiful flames.

I'm cold.

"Fia," James says, and I love the way he always answers the phone with my name: a statement, not a question.

"So, here's the thing about Sadie."

"Sadie?"

I slap my forehead, swear. "Did your father not tell you? I'm in Florida with the brain leech. We found Sadie."

"He didn't tell me." There's a pause, and I can feel his worry seeping across the miles and miles and miles of empty air between us. "But I haven't talked to him yet today. I'm sure he would have mentioned it."

"Mmm." I lie back, the concrete of the sidewalk hard and baking hot through my T-shirt, but it's not hot enough. I squeeze my eyes shut against the sun, let it burn my eyes through my eyelids. I once stared at the sun as long as I could, trying to go blind like Annie. Maybe if it had worked, we would still be together, be safe, be worthless to evil men and therefore free to just be.

James prods me. "Are you still there?"

"There's something wrong. Sadie's only a Seer, but . . ." But why is she special? Why was she so important? Seers aren't super useful in general. There's no reason she should keep popping up on the radar like this.

"Is . . . anyone else with her?"

He doesn't say the name. He doesn't know that Pixie knows that Annie isn't dead. The tightrope I walk keeps stretching, with no end in view. Farther and farther from my goal.

"No. I'd know if she were here again." I would. I would know that, I'd have to.

I tap tap tap tap. Tap tap tap tap. Tap tap tap tap. What is so important about Sadie? There is something I'm not realizing, some huge piece I'm failing to put together, and that failure scares me. I can't fail. Sadie shouldn't be dangerous, shouldn't set off my warning bells. I bring all sorts of girls in. Sure, she has a history of triggering bloodshed (four, four taps, I hate them), but she's just a Seer. Seers are lame. They can't control what they see or when they see it.

"*Oh.*" It's an exhalation, a curse and a prayer and a eulogy. Because I understand now. What she is. What she means. Seers can't see me, none except Annie. I'm too slippery, I slide right out of their visions.

Sadie looked at Pixie's hand and thought she didn't want to see that future. She knew she would. There was no question.

"She touches you," I whisper, "and she sees. That's all she needs. She touches you. She touches *anyone.* She can control what she sees."

"What is—" He stops and I know he's made the same connection, the connection I can't think about with Pixie next to me, the great new kink to all our not planning. Because if someone could force a vision, if someone could grab hold of your future and force it into her brain with a simple brush of her finger across your skin, nothing would be secret.

Nothing would be safe.

Nothing.

I can already feel all my secrets, the secrets from James, the secrets from his father, the secrets from everyone, spilling out in a torrent, gushing past my skin and into someone else, and I wouldn't be able to stop them. There would be no dam for the flood, no way around it, no place to hide.

Sadie is my death warrant. James's, too.

"Is Mae with you?" James asks.

"Yes."

"Get away from her. Now."

I stand. Pixie looks up, but I jab a finger at her and think *STAY* as hard as I can, then run the opposite direction. I don't know what her range is, so I give us a couple of blocks.

"Okay," I say. "I can think now."

"My father can't get Sadie."

"I agree."

"No, I mean, my father *cannot* get her. Absolutely cannot. Under no circumstances. She would destroy everything, Fia. We'd be ruined."

I walk in tight circles, needing to move, needing to run, needing needing but never getting. "I know. *I know.*"

"What are we going to do?"

"It'll be fine. I'll tell him Sadie is a dead end, a Seer of so little talent she isn't worth the hassle of taking. I'll tell him Lerner already ditched her."

"Mae knows what she can do."

I kick a mailbox post, one two three four times. "I'll talk to her. She'll do what I ask."

"She isn't on our side."

"She's on *my* side. She's my friend."

"Fia, her job is to monitor you!"

"What? No. *My* job is to monitor *her*!"

His voice goes soft, gentle. "She's doing exactly what my father wanted me to do. He keeps me busy and away from you, while she takes all your free time, goes out with you, listens to you. She got past your defenses. She's working for him. He never doubted her. He doubted you."

No. No no no no. I couldn't be this wrong, not about someone. If I am this wrong about Pixie, what about James? "You did the same thing, you did everything he asked you to. Are you telling me you didn't really like me? Don't really love me?"

"Of course I love you!"

"Then why couldn't she? Why is it so impossible that she'd be loyal to me, really be my friend?" I hang my head, ashamed of the hot tears sliding down my cheeks. She's my friend. She is. I know she is. I would know if she weren't. Wouldn't I?

"That's not what I'm saying."

"It is. And you're right. No one who could hear my thoughts would want to be around me. Not even you." She must hate me, she has to hate me. She's one of them.

"Shh. Stop. I know you, Fia, and I love you." His voice is

fierce, and fierce James is my biggest comfort. "All I'm saying is, you have to be sure she won't tell. Are you sure?"

I wipe my face, miserable and alone. So very alone. All I have is James. He's the only one I can trust. "What did you find in North Dakota?" I ask, stalling.

His voice is dark and strained. "Another complication. I'll tell you later when you're free to think. You decide what to do about the Sadie situation. Fast. And then call me. Do not talk to my father or anyone from Keane until you've called me."

"Okay."

"And don't kill Mae yet," he says casually, like it's an afterthought. "We can only get away with that so many times."

"I—" The line is dead. I turn back toward where I left Pixie, the "yet" echoing in my skull.

I am not lost, I never get lost, my sense of direction is perfect, but oh, I am so very very lost. I drift back toward the sidewalk where I left Pixie. She's sitting, legs tucked under her chin. She doesn't look up as I sit next to her.

I don't know what to think. Not for myself and not for her.

"We can't take her back with us," I say.

"All right."

"We have to lie about why."

"All right."

"Really? Just like that?"

She pushes her sunglasses on top of her bleached hair and looks at me. Her eyes are dark, rich brown. It's the first time I've actually noticed their color behind all the eye makeup. They're pretty. I like them.

"Just like that," she says. "I trust your decision."

I hang my head and laugh. "Why?"

"Because when we were on a sidewalk ringed with men holding guns, you only thought about getting me out safe. I don't trust you to take care of yourself, but I trust you to take care of me. And I trust you to take care of her." She jerks her head in the direction of Sadie's house.

"What if all this is me taking care of me?" I whisper.

"You wouldn't even begin to know how." She stands and holds a hand out to help me.

I take it.

I hope James is wrong. But I don't know. I don't know how to feel a friendship. I only ever had Annie, and what we have is so much more than friendship. Is this how friends feel, this give-and-take, this sharp fear tempered with hope?

"Let's call for a pickup at that café. It's too freaking green out here." Pixie glares at the spiky grass and abundant, bright flowers around us like they are personally offensive, then replaces her sunglasses as a shield against nature.

I take a step to follow her but

There is something

Something big

Something very very big very very wrong so wrong—

I turn in time to see a large white van with no windows pull into Sadie's driveway. Two men get out and walk straight up the front porch and into the house without knocking.

"Pixie," I say, but I don't wait for her to respond, I sprint. Wrong wrong wrong wrong, I have to get there first, I have to stop them.

I'm five houses away. The driver rolls down his window and meets my eyes. I know him. How do I know him?

Sandy blond with the gun! The one who worked with Lerner!

Someone slams into me from behind, tackling me to the sidewalk. I roll, pulling my attacker with me and pinning the person to the ground, my forearm against a throat. Pixie's throat. Why?

"Stop!" she gasps. "Stop! You have to stop! He's thinking about Annie! If you take Sadie, they'll hurt her. He knows I can hear him, he's telling me what he'll do to her, it's . . . oh please please stop." She sobs, and I lean back, watching as the two men who went inside walk out with Sadie, holding her elbows. She doesn't fight them, but hangs her head as though she's being marched to the gallows.

Sandy blond with the gun smiles at me, tips his head.

"I'll kill you," I scream, and I mean it, I do, I will kill him I will I will I will.

He laughs. Closes the door. Backs out of the driveway and drives right past us, because he can, and I can't do a thing to stop him.

ANNIE

Four Weeks Before

COLE LETS OUT A LONG, LOW STRING OF SWEARWORDS. "There's a Bentley parked in front of her house. They're already here, it has to be them."

My stomach sinks. They're right there, right inside. That monster, James, and Eden—whom I miss so much it hurts. Why is she still working with them?

I snap. "Wait! What time is it? Sarah, look up where her school is! In the vision, she got home after James and Eden were already there. Then Fia came a few minutes after Sadie walked in. So it was James and Eden, then Sadie, then Fia."

"Adam needs to stop texting me," she mutters. He was desperate to come when he found out it involved Fia, but Rafael agreed it was best for just the three of us to make this trip. "Okay, go two blocks east and pull over. The high school gets out in five minutes, and she's close enough she'll probably walk. This will put us right in her way, unless she goes a strange route home."

Cole parks and we get out of the car. I tell them again what Sadie is wearing, though we've gone over the vision so much we all know every detail.

I lean against a wall, my cane in the car so we don't draw attention in case there are any other Keane employees out and about. Eden is right down the street. James is right down the street.

And Fia is here, somewhere.

I wish we could abandon Sadie and kidnap Fia instead.

"Sadie?" Sarah says, and I stand up straight.

"Yeah?" The girl sounds wary.

Sarah actually starts crying. "We did it. We found you first. I didn't think we would."

"I need to go home."

"You can't," I say. "There are people there. Bad people." Eden isn't bad. Fia isn't bad. She's not, she's not. "They want to take you to a private school. They'll say it's to help you, but they want to take advantage of you, use you for your abilities."

"What abilities?" Her voice is cautious, with an edge of fear.

"Do you see things? Things that haven't happened yet? Or maybe you can feel what other people feel. Or know what they're thinking without them telling you."

I can hear her breathing getting faster and uneven. "I—no. No. I can't. No. I have to go home. My mom wouldn't send me to the school. They invited me already, and we said no."

"She's going to sign the papers, Sadie. I've already seen it. I went to the school. Please believe me that you want to stay as far away from it as you can."

"She said—my mom said—no, I'll go tell her." I feel the air shift as she walks by me and I am so desperate to keep her here, away from that house, that I reach out for her. If she goes home, if she meets Fia, we have lost our chance forever, I know it. I put my arm out too high, though, and my hand brushes her neck, her hair tangling in my fingers.

"Sadie, wait, please—"

She stumbles, then something bangs on the car hood next to us.

"Sadie? Are you okay?" Sarah asks.

"She's having a seizure." Cole grunts, then I hear the car door opening.

"What are you doing?" I ask, my hands fluttering uselessly in the empty space in front of me.

"I'm putting her in the car. We're exposed here, and if she seizes for too long, we need to get to a hospital fast."

I wait, frozen, in the middle of the sidewalk. This is all a mess. It's broken. We were supposed to convince her. I wanted to kidnap Fia, not Sadie. "What if she still wants to go home?"

Sarah answers. "It's not up to her anymore. Cole, take care of her. There's one more piece we have to fix." She grabs my arm, starts pulling me down the sidewalk.

"Did you see something?" Cole shouts.

"I saw everything," Sarah says, an unfamiliar ragged edge to her voice, but it's so quiet I'm sure Cole couldn't hear her.

"Where are we going?"

"Fia shows up after Sadie, right?"

"Yes."

"Well, don't you want to talk to her?"

"Of course, but is that a good idea? She's with James, and—"

"Oh, I am very well aware that she's with James. We'll wait next to the house. She'll know we're there. Her perfect instincts will tell her something is wrong."

Sarah's going too fast, and I stumble several times trying to keep up. After a few minutes she pushes me against a splintered wooden fence. I rub my arm where her fingers dug in so hard I can feel bruises.

"Sarah, please tell me what's going on."

Her footsteps continue in front of me, back and forth, pacing. I think she's whispering to herself, but I can't make out the words.

And then she says, "Well hello, Fia. So nice of you to join us."

"Fia?" I stand up straight, holding out a trembling hand. Fia's here. She's *right here*.

"What are you doing?" Fia hisses, and it feels like a slap in the face.

"We're saving Sadie."

"No, Annie, what are you doing here? You can't be here! You're dead, you have to be dead! I thought she'd be safe with you! What are you thinking, bringing her where you know Keane's people are?"

There's a metallic click. Sarah's voice sounds calmer than it has for the last few weeks. "You need to stop."

"You have the safety on," Fia says. "If you're going to point a gun at me, take the safety off first."

"You're pointing a gun at her? Are you crazy?" I grab for where Sarah was, and then she's behind me, her arm around my neck, the barrel of the gun against my temple.

"You have to stop," she says again.

"I can't," Fia whispers, and she doesn't sound scared. I'm scared. I'm so scared I can't move. "I have to finish it or all this . . . everything is meaningless. Put the gun down."

"You think you're the only one willing to go that far? If it means stopping you, I'll do it. I'll do anything."

"It's not about Fia," I say, swallowing and swallowing against the pressure at my throat. "It's about Keane. Put the gun down, Sarah."

"Do you see Keane anywhere? Because I don't! All I see is Fia, snatching girl after girl after girl before I can save them.

Do you know what else I see? Broken girls floating lifeless in a river. So many. All the ones that fail him. I don't see anything else, not anymore. Every vision, every time, dead girls. And she is *helping* him. She is making him so much stronger than he used to be. If I have to see one more body, one more pair of blank eyes—I won't. I can't. I know you, Fia. You're not untouchable. You need Annie safe in order to function." Her arm tightens, and the barrel digs into my skin. "Well, she's not safe anymore."

"Please," I whisper. How did I not see this coming? How could we not notice how unhinged Sarah had become?

"I'll give you a choice. Kneel on the ground and let me kill you, or I'll kill Annie. Either one will finish this. You or Annie. It's that simple."

"Nothing is simple," Fia says, her voice dead.

"THIS IS. Choose. Now. Or I'll kill her."

"I'm sorry," Fia whispers.

I nearly jump out of my skin at the next voice. Eden. "Fia, where have you— What the hell? *Annie*?"

"You can't see Annie," Fia says, dreamy and distracted. "You can't know she's alive. It's all ruined. I have to fix it."

There's a soft gasp behind me and the gun moves away from my temple, the arm around my neck loosens. Sarah leans heavily against my back.

"No," I shout, lunging forward to block Fia with my body, but she's not there. Sarah falls to the ground behind me. "Fia? Fia, where are you?"

"I'm sorry, I'm sorry, I'm sorry."

Eden is moaning something to God, over and over, but I don't need God, I need Fia. I spin, trying to find her, then notice the back of my shirt is wet. I touch it, and my fingers come away slick with something thicker than water.

"Sarah?" I ask, already knowing she won't answer.

Fia's voice brings back nightmares of empty pill bottles. "I can't do this again, I can't, I can't, no no no no, no no no no."

I hold out my hands, one covered in Sarah's blood, the other clean. "Fia, come here. Come here. Let's leave, right now. It's okay. We'll leave."

A door slams somewhere nearby and I wander in small circles trying to find my sister. I nearly trip on something, and bile rises in my throat as I realize it's an arm. Sarah's arm.

"Fia," James says, and I freeze.

"She was going to kill Annie," she says. "I had to. I— James, please, please, make it better, fix it, fix me, please please please." Her breath hitches and a sob chokes out.

I have my hands out in nothing but open space. She doesn't come to me.

"It's going to be fine," James says. "Go get in the car. I'll be there in a minute. Everything is going to be fine."

I wait for her to disagree with him, to say something to me, anything, but she simply says, "Okay."

And then she's gone.

"You just couldn't stay dead, could you, Annie?"

"I—I didn't know this would happen." Fia left me. Again.

"Of course you didn't. When do you ever?" He sighs heavily. "Now what I am supposed to do with this?"

I recoil in horror. "*This* is a girl named Sarah." She was my friend. She would have killed me or Fia. I don't know how to feel. I will never know how to feel again.

Eden's voice shakes. "Will someone please explain this to me? You were dead— I saw you, she killed you, I saw it. You were *dead*." She pulls me to her and smashes me in a hug.

James sounds annoyed. "You'll never be able to keep this quiet in your head. This whole trip is a wash. Fine. Eden, congratulations, Fia killed you for double-crossing us and alerting Lerner so they got to Sadie first. You can join Annie in death, and please for the love of all that is holy, *stay away from us*. I'm calling for a cleanup guy who won't tell my father it's the wrong body, and I suggest you both run. Now."

"Go to hell," Eden spits, then takes my hand and pulls me down the sidewalk, away from the blood, away from the body, away from my sister, once again broken because of me.

I didn't even get to talk to her.

I didn't even get to touch her.

And James will fill in the holes in her soul, drawing her even closer to him and further and further away from me.

"There's a car," I manage to say after a couple of minutes. "Cole—I don't know where he is."

"Brown hair, running down the sidewalk toward us, looks like he's going to murder me?"

"Annie? Annie!" Cole grabs me around the shoulders, twisting me away from Eden's hand. "She said—Sadie woke up and said you were dead. She said Sarah was going to—I thought I'd be too late, I thought I'd lose you." He pulls me close, holding me tighter than even Eden did. "Where's Sarah?"

"She's gone," I whisper. I have nothing else to say.

FIA

Twelve Hours Before

~

"AND YOU'RE CERTAIN IT WAS THE LERNER GROUP who grabbed Sadie? And you couldn't stop them?" the Feeler asks. She's new. I don't know her. I don't care.

I nod, channeling anger, which isn't hard. I am angry. I am so angry I don't know what to do with it. I wanted to help her, wanted to keep Sadie safe. I was going to keep her safe, but I couldn't.

I couldn't fix it.

I couldn't do anything to change what happened.

I don't tell her why we couldn't stop them. That they threatened to hurt Annie so we couldn't save Sadie. Because Annie is dead, SHE IS DEAD WHY IS EVERYTHING SO COMPLICATED SHE IS DEAD.

I frown, realizing the Feeler has been asking more questions. "Look. I recognized the guy. Sandy blond hair, face I want to smash. I fought him last spring when I was out on a hit, and then again when Lerner kidnapped me and I broke out. I don't forget people I beat the crap out of."

"No, I would imagine you don't." I don't know if her smile is amused or terrified, and I don't care. I'm done.

I stand and stomp out of the room. The one bonus to all this is that we didn't have to lie. Pixie and I decided not to tell them exactly what Sadie could do, just that we saw the tail end of her being forced into a car and couldn't stop it.

Couldn't.

COULDN'T.

I *hate* couldn't. I hate it so much I want to hurt someone. I want to hurt Sandy blond who threatened Annie. I want to hurt everyone associated with the Lerner group, everyone I trusted. I trusted them! It was right to trust them! And trusting them meant Sarah died, meant she was destroyed. Trusting them means Sadie still isn't safe, won't ever be safe.

I gave Annie to them. Maybe even to Rafael, if he wasn't lying.

I gave Annie to *Rafael.* No I didn't. I KILLED ANNIE. I KILLED HER.

I walk into the women's bathroom. Kick a stall door so hard it cracks.

Scream.

Slam the heel of my palm into the mirror, watch it shatter, watch my reflection break into pieces. A slivered and silvered distortion, all broken and jagged and ruined.

"Fia!"

I turn to see Pixie staring at me. I don't know how long she's been in here. "Fia," she says, her voice careful. "You need to calm down, okay?"

"I'm calm," I answer, raising an eyebrow at her. "Why wouldn't I be calm?"

"It'll be okay."

I laugh, and it is broken and jagged like the mirror. "No big deal. I'm pissed because this failure will probably cost me employee of the year. I really wanted a plaque. My name etched on it next to a bad picture."

She opens her mouth, and I want to shove my bloodied hand over it, want to smash her into the wall, want to keep her from saying whatever soft things she wants to say. She is just like Annie. She is a liar. She will tell me and tell me and tell me and tell me that everything will be okay, and it's a lie, it's always a lie.

She takes a step back, pain and hurt written around her eyes. She wears leather and metal armor, but she's a kid. She's a stupid kid, and she doesn't understand any of this and she doesn't know anything, she doesn't know.

She can never know.

Actually, no. If she stays here long enough, she'll know. She'll know, and then she'll be the broken doll she already looks like. You want to play here, Pixie? You want to know what it really means to be a part of all this? You want thoughts to pull out of my head and report back to Keane? I'll give you thoughts.

She leans against the black-tiled wall, stares past me at the shattered mirror. "There's an artist in Asheville, where I'm from. She works in mosaic. Takes broken pieces of mirrors and fits them back into patterns. I have one. It looks like a starburst, the pieces rearranged to shine outward like rays of light."

I narrow my eyes. "It's still a broken mirror. It's ruined. It's useless."

She shrugs, still not looking at me. "It's broken, yeah. But it's beautiful. And it means something to me when I look at it, even if I can't see myself clearly in it anymore."

I'm overwhelmed with the impulse to go over to her, to let her hug me, to cry on her shoulder. Is it an instinct? Is it right? Is it wrong?

"I'm on your side," she says, smiling sadly. "You're the only friend I have."

I pick up one of the thick, folded paper towels. Smear my blood across it, wad it into a ball, and drop it in the sink. I don't trust this impulse, I don't trust her, I don't trust me. No. I only trust me. No. I am the last person I can trust. I am the only person I can trust. I tap tap tap tap a fingernail against the sink, consider the spiderweb of my reflection.

"Here's the thing, Pixie. I don't have a side. I work here. *Just like you.* And I don't ever forget that." My phone rings, and I pull it out of my pocket. James. James will know what to do. He'll tell me. We'll do it together.

"Please," Pixie says, desperate. "If I wanted to hurt you, I'd have already done it. You gave your secrets away before I ever listened in your head and realized you haven't killed the people you say you did. Tap tap tap tap, Fia. Four taps. But you've *killed* six people. Two with the bomb. Clarice. Adam. Annie. Eden. It wouldn't even be my word against yours. All they'd have to do is look and they'd see the truth."

I cock my head, consider. She's right. I could laugh at how careless I've been. "Are you threatening me?"

"No! I'm telling you to be more careful! I care about you. But James is destroying you. He lets you think you have the same goals, but he wants nothing that you do. He was working with Rafael, building his own group to rival his father's. He has been this entire time, playing Lerner, playing his father, building so that he can take over and create the *exact same thing* his father already has. He's not going to stop anything. You're just building an empire for a new Keane."

I have her slammed up against the wall before she can blink.

"You know nothing," I snarl. *Nothing. You know nothing, and you are nothing, and you mean nothing to me or anyone else. No one in the whole world cares about you. I say a word, a single word, and you are the next overdosed girl floating dead in the river.*

She whimpers.

I lean my forehead against hers, close my eyes. My voice comes out even, soft. "Stay out of it. I really don't want to hurt you."

I leave the bathroom before she can read me, before she can realize that I am lying, that I am nothing but a lie. I do, I care, I care so much and it terrifies me, and I don't want to care about her because when I care people get hurt.

The people we love are the ones with the power to destroy us.

James is all I have. I chose James. He has to be right. Please let him be right.

ANNIE

Twenty-eight Days Before

~

WE SIT, A SILENT, MISERABLE GROUP. THE HOTEL SUITE has adjoining rooms, and the walls are thin enough to make out most of what Rafael and Cole are shouting at each other. I had been worried about what would happen when I saw Rafael again after our kiss, but it's funny how trivial something like that is now.

As much as I want to mourn Sarah, part of me is livid. I'm furious with her, furious that she made those choices, that she forced Fia's hand like that. I have no idea what this will do to my sister.

No, that's wrong. I know exactly what this will do, and this time I'm not there to take care of her. Please, James. Whatever goodness you have in you, whatever humanity—please take care of Fia. Don't let her hurt herself.

"I just don't understand," Adam says, anguish soaking his voice. "Why would Sarah do that?"

"She was on amphetamines, right?" Eden asks. She's sitting next to me, and I'm curled into her, my head resting on her shoulder.

She told me she stayed because they threatened to kill her mom. It was the hardest choice she'd ever had to make, because she loved me more than she ever loved her mom, and betraying my memory to protect that woman was torture. But now that Eden's dead, too, we can be together. I shouldn't be so grateful, considering everything that was lost for this to happen, but I won't let Eden go again.

It took us a few days of hotel hopping before we all got to the same place and felt safe enough to meet. Sadie has barely spoken five words to any of us. She also hasn't showered, and I can smell her from across the room. Someone needs to take care of her, help her, but we're all so shell-shocked by what happened. At least she seems calm and resigned to being with us.

Eden continues. "I've seen some of our girls on it. It can make you paranoid, even trigger brief psychotic episodes."

Apparently Cole feels the same, given the accusations he's hurling at Rafael.

"Get away from her," Eden snaps.

"What?" Nathan says. I wish he weren't here.

"Don't get anywhere near Sadie. She doesn't want you to."

"I think she can talk for herself."

"I think you can take a flying leap off the balcony for all I care. Just stay away from her, you're making her nervous."

Nathan mutters something under his breath, but we're interrupted by the door opening.

"Well," Rafael says, his voice artificially bright. "We've got to decide what to do next. Obviously we can't all stay together. Adam, it's easiest if you're with me. So, Cole, you and Eden can take Sadie to a safe house, and I'll take Adam and Annie."

"No." Sadie's voice is lower than I expect it to be, almost husky. "I want to stay with Annie."

I'm surprised by this, but pleased. Someone needs to take care of her, so I'll be that someone. It's about time I had someone to take care of again. "Okay," I say.

Rafael sounds patient as he's talking to Sadie, but something is off. "I don't think it's safe for you and me to be in the same location, since they might be looking for us. Why don't you explain exactly what you can do, and we can decide where the best place is for you."

Then it hits me. Rafael uses a different tone of voice when he's talking to women. His accent masked it, and, if I'm being honest, I liked flirting with him too much to notice. It's not obviously condescending and skeezy like Nathan, but it's there.

That detail feels like sand on my skin, irritating and

impossible to brush away. "It's okay. I'll go with Sadie."

Eden takes my hand and draws casually in my palm. I wonder what she's doing until I realize she's forming letters.

What is wrong?

"Eden, can you show me where the bathroom is?" I ask.

She stands, taking my arm, and leads me through a room. We close the door behind ourselves. "You're worried. What?"

"I don't know. I'm confused. I'm so worried about Fia. And I don't know how to feel about things here. Rafael is . . . I don't think I had him figured out the way I thought I did."

"Yeah, he's a puzzle. You were distracted by his accent, weren't you?"

I laugh. "Shut up. Okay, yes. I was. Listen, I'll stay with Sadie. I feel responsible, you know? But I worry about Adam."

"He seems like a good guy."

"He is. But . . ." I tell her about the vision that started all this. "I think he needs to be watched. Would you—this is awful, I don't want to be separated from you, but would you stay with him?"

She sighs. "I just barely got you back. But this is important to you. I'll do it. And I'll try to feel out Rafael better."

I hug her. "Thank you."

"Seriously though, this company is wasted on you. Adam is all nerd hot, Rafael has that whole Latin lover vibe going, and even Cole is smoking. It's kind of a slow build, you know? At first he looks pretty average, but then he's got this incredible intensity in his stares, and his body is *rocking*. I should have joined Lerner ages ago."

I laugh. "You'll get no argument on that point. I'm so, so glad you are here."

"Me, too. But they're going to start wondering why you need so much help in the bathroom. I'll head back and volunteer to stick with Adam and Rafael. Rafael thinks I'm very attractive—which I am, obviously—so he won't have an issue with it."

"Wait, when you said you were going to try to feel out Rafael better, did you mean emotionally, or did you mean literally?"

Her laugh is downright evil as she closes the door and leaves me in the bathroom.

Already missing her, I follow a few minutes later.

"I go with Annie and Sadie," Cole says.

"I think you've earned a vacation," Rafael says. "After what happened to Sarah. I know how close you two were. Nathan can get Annie and Sadie to a safe house."

"No!" My response is too strong and too fast, but I can't help it. "No offense, Nathan, but I don't like you."

"Why would that offend me?" he asks, voice dark.

"I'd rather be with Cole. Is that okay, Sadie?"

She doesn't answer.

"Is it?"

"She's nodding," Eden says. "Sweetie, you've got to remember to say yes or no. Okay. I feel like we should have a team cheer or something." She pulls me into a hug and I squeeze her as tight as I can.

"Take care of yourself," she says.

"You, too."

Adam gives me a quick hug, and then Rafael gives me a much less quick hug. "Are you sure?" he whispers against my ear.

"I'm sure. I owe it to Sadie."

"Okay. I'll see you soon."

"Let's get going," Cole says. He takes my elbow and the three of us walk out of the room.

I try to broach the subject as casually as I can while Cole is out buying food and supplies. "Hey, Sadie, you want the first shower?" It's been a week since we left Rafael and co., and we've been traveling in a random pattern, never deciding beforehand where we'll go. Cole wants to give us a few weeks of unpredictability before we settle at a safe house.

Sadie has not showered once.

I've tried to draw her out into conversation to no avail. She's like traveling with a ghost. A ghost with BO.

"I can't," she whispers.

"What do you mean?"

"I don't have my gloves."

I frown. "You need gloves for the shower?"

"I can't touch myself."

"I'm sorry. I really don't understand."

"When I touch myself, I see things. It hurts. I don't want to see them. I had shower gloves at home, so I wasn't touching my own skin. It's not as bad as when I touch other people, but it's still too much."

I sit on the bed across from her. "Wait, you see things when you touch people?"

"Yes."

"So when I touched your face . . ."

"She killed you." Sadie moves closer, her voice getting more intense. "She killed you—I saw it. And then that other girl, the one who looks like you, killed her. The things I see, they never change. Never. So how come you're not dead?"

I smile sadly. "That other girl? She's my sister. Fia has a way of changing things. She can't help it. Nothing's ever set in stone where Fia's concerned."

"So your visions . . ."

I shrug. "They aren't always right. Sometimes I see them wrong. Sometimes they change."

"It's not fate, then. What you see." Hope lightens her voice, just a bit.

"I don't think so. And I'll get you some shower mitts. When you need things, please ask. If anyone understands weird requests, it's us."

She's quiet, and then she hurriedly says, "I'm nodding. Thank you."

When Cole returns, Sadie's made a list for him, and he goes right back out. By the time he's finished it's late, but the shower is running and I collapse on the bed, relieved. "Oh, thank goodness. Being in a car with her was horrible. Poor little thing."

Cole sighs, and I feel the bed shift as he sits next to me. "Every time she touches anyone? Including herself?"

"Yup. Sucks to be her."

His breathing slows, gets even, and I think he's falling asleep. I take a pillow and start sliding off the bed, but his hand shoots out and grabs my wrist. "I'll take the floor," he says.

"I'm sorry."

"I don't mind."

"I'm sorry for so much more. I know how stressed out I make you. And—" My throat catches. "I'm so sorry about Sarah. I can't help feeling like it was my fault. Please don't tell me it wasn't."

Cole's voice comes out softer than I've ever heard it. There's no edge, none of the sharp steel and stone I know in it. "I'm sorry about her, too. But it wasn't your fault."

He lets go of my wrist and moves to the floor. Lying on the bed, I have a sudden, overwhelming urge to crawl off and curl up next to him. It hits me how much I've come to depend on him, but it's different than it was with Fia. I feel like depending on him makes me stronger, not more helpless.

"Thank you," I whisper, and the words hang on the air between us. It's not enough, but I can't figure out how to voice anything else.

By the time Sadie comes out I'm half asleep, but the scent of shampoo and soap makes me smile as I drift off.

I'm woken as light bursts behind my eyes.

In the vision, Sadie is on a black leather couch in a window-lined room. There's a glass door open to a balcony overlooking a skyscraper-filled skyline. She's curled into the corner of the couch, legs tucked protectively in front of her chest. Her face is empty as she stares at the floor.

A heavy door opens and two people enter the room. One, carefully handsome James, something tight and frightened around his eyes but not showing in his broad smile.

The other is Phillip Keane.

And then a third person comes in and my heart twists to see Fia, my Fia, but something is wrong with her. She looks from Sadie to Phillip Keane and back again, slides along the wall next to the door. James gives her a sharp, expectant expression.

The line of her eyes shifts them into a shape I don't recognize.

Something is very, *very* wrong with Fia.

Phillip Keane smiles his soulless robot smile, and says, "Hello, Sadie."

Fia spasms once, twice, as though she can't quite move. Then she pushes Phillip Keane out of the way, jumps in front of Sadie, and stabs her in the chest.

Sadie looks down, her eyes sad but not surprised.

"She was going to—" Fia stands up straight, drops the knife. "She was going to—kill— she was going to kill . . ." Fia looks back at James, her blue eyes pleading and impossibly sad, and then something in them dies. Fia's expression drops away and she drifts to the balcony.

"Fia?" James says, his voice tight with panic.

Fia climbs onto the stone railing and jumps off.

FIA

Eleven Hours Before

~

I DON'T CALL JAMES UNTIL I'M OUT ON THE SIDEWALK, weaving through the masses of people, losing my security tail without much effort.

"Why didn't you answer?" He sounds panicked.

"I was in the middle of something."

"We're dead. It's over."

I stop where I am; someone cusses me out as they almost walk into me but I don't care. Pixie. Pixie betrayed us. It feels wrong, I should have felt it, should have known. I am broken.

James is still talking. "—my father agreed to a meeting. He says Rafael Marino contacted him, said he has a Seer who can force visions on demand. *Rafael.*" He swears, and I should be surprised but I'm not. Rafael is definitely Lerner, then. Pixie didn't betray us.

I betrayed her.

Better sooner than later.

"But you two were working together," I say as calmly as I can.

There's a pause, a pause I can fill with James scrambling to decide what lie to fill this hole with. He can't. There are too many holes, their edges are all meeting up, it's too big now.

"Did Mae tell you that? She's a liar, Fia. She's trying to come between us. I hate Rafael, you know that. I should have killed him when I had the chance," James says. "But it's Sadie he's got, it has to be." The subject change is not lost on me. "He's bringing her in, trying to make some sort of deal. The meeting is already set; my father called me to come back for it. If he gets her, it's all over."

I push someone to the side, force my way to where I can lean up against the streetlamp-lit exterior of a building. I close my eyes, try to feel it out, but I can't feel anything. I'm dead inside. "We can work around it."

"We can't! There are too many things we're already hiding. I know where Adam is."

"Adam?" Gray eyes. Sweet and gentle Adam. Safe and hidden Adam. Safe and hidden like Annie. Both with Lerner, both with Rafael, who has been playing this whole thing for months while I've been running around mindlessly, not even knowing the game I was losing.

NOTHINGICANCONTROLNOTHINGNOTHING NOTHING.

James talks fast, and I can hear the rhythm in his voice from his pacing. "Adam was my big North Dakota surprise. He was working in a custom lab, set up by Rafael. Apparently Annie and Eden were living nearby, but he wouldn't say where and I didn't have time to find them. All your dead friends in one place. I tried to call Rafael and bargain, using Adam as leverage, but he wouldn't answer. He doesn't need him now that he has Sadie. I can only hide so many things before a Feeler or a Reader or a Seer catches us. And if Sadie comes in, we won't be able to hide anything at all."

I sink down the side of the wall, sit on the sidewalk. "What do we do?"

There's a pause, a long pause, a pause I fill with wondering what Adam and James talk about. It would be funny, really, picturing them in a conversation any other time. They could talk about brains. Compare notes about whether I'm a good kisser. Rafael could join that conversation, too. Or maybe they'd just play video games.

"I have an idea," James says, and everything in my head explodes with wrong, wrong, wrong, wrong. I am sick with it, lost to gravity, unmoored. I dig my toes into the concrete, try to curl them into the ground through my shoes.

"Fia, are you still there?"

"Yes," I whisper.

"We're in this together. Forever. This is the only way we can do this. We're close, we're on the edge, we just need a little more time. A little more time and we'll be done."

James. My James. He is the only person I have left. Pixie said . . . Pixie lied. James is ending this, not starting it again. A little more time.

"And this is the only way to make sure Annie stays safe," he adds. "My father can't know she's alive."

"Yes," I whisper again.

"You have to kill Sadie."

The tapping in my skull is so loud I don't know if I heard him right. "I have to kill Sadie," I repeat.

"Yes. It's the only way. Now that my father knows Sadie exists, he'll never stop until he has her. And we already have the answer with what you did when Casey tried to kill him. Tomorrow, during the meeting. He trusts you, trusts your instincts. You kill Sadie, slip a weapon into her clothes, and then tell him you had the same feeling. You had a feeling that she was going to try to kill him. Tell him Rafael set it all up. It'll be easy."

"It'll be easy." I think I'm laughing. Am I laughing? Someone pauses, hovers above me, asks if I'm okay. I can't look up, can't stop laughing, can't breathe.

"Go to the hotel. I'll be home in two hours. Don't talk to *anyone*, and stay away from the office."

The tapping gets louder and I want to get out of my head, need to get out of my head. I picture a drill going through my skull, making a hole to release the pressure from the tapping the tap tap tap tapping the tap tap tap tapping that never stops.

"I can't." The words slam out of me, a desperate gasp. "I can't, James."

"You can. It's to protect Annie. You've killed to protect Annie before. This is the same thing. If you don't do this, the other deaths have no meaning. No reason."

"Not like this . . . I didn't walk into a room knowing I was about to kill an innocent girl. I didn't want to, I never wanted to, I never planned to . . . James, I never planned to. I didn't think. If I could go back, if I could undo them, if . . ."

Clarice's dead eyes, soft Sarah's brown eyes, they've never stopped staring at me, they'll never stop staring at me. I chose that. I didn't want to choose it, I didn't think about it, but I chose it.

I can't choose this, I can't I can't I can't.

"You can't go back. You can never go back. And this is the only way to go forward."

"Please," I say, and I am definitely not laughing I am crying, "Please don't ask me to do this."

There's a long silence, and I think he's crying with me. I want him to be. "Fia, love. You chose me. You chose us. That was the right choice. You make the choices you need to, because you are strong when no one else is. You make the hard choices."

I nod. I chose him. If I chose him, he had to be the right choice. I wouldn't love him if it weren't right.

"This is the only way for us. You have to do this. For us, for my mother, for every girl my father has hurt. To save all the ones he will hurt. We'll save them."

To save them. To save Annie. To save Adam. To save James. Kill Sadie to save them.

"Okay," a voice says, and I think it's mine.

"Okay. Okay. We'll be okay. Go home. I'll be there as soon as I can. We're going to be okay, Fia. I love you."

"Okay." I lower my phone and stare at the screen. It goes black, and I can see my reflection. It's wrong. I stand, drop my phone on the sidewalk, grind my heel into it until it cracks. Better.

No other options. No other options. I drift along the streets, not thinking, not planning. We shouldn't have talked about it as much as we did. I will plan nothing. I grab a phone out of the diaper bag of a woman trying to console a screaming toddler. I don't know why until I'm dialing the number I have memorized from the card he gave me.

I need another option. Any other option. The phone rings.

"Hello?"

"Rafael," I say, closing my eyes against the sick swirl of wrong that leeches the color out of everything around me. There is no right choice, not for me, not now. Maybe there never was. "You said we wanted the same thing. What do we want?"

I can hear the slick triumphant smile in his voice. "We want to keep your sister safe."

"And how do we do that?"

"By doing exactly what I tell you."

I listen.

ANNIE

Seven Days Before

~

"PHONE FOR YOU," SADIE CHIRPS THROUGH THE door. "It's Eden."

"I'm in the bathtub."

"I promise not to look. I hate skin."

I laugh, and she opens the door, putting the phone in my outstretched hand. The gloves she's wearing are soft, but she's got to be burning up in them all the time.

"You're going to miss the winner of the cake decorating contest," she says.

"Well, pay lots of attention so you can describe it to me in great detail when I get out."

"Will do." She closes the door behind herself, humming happily.

"Hey, Eden," I say, cradling the phone against my ear, every part of me exhausted and worn down from the last two weeks of running.

"How you holding up?"

"Fine."

"Liar. I don't have to Feel you to know you're crumbling."

I lean my head against the back of the bath, running my fingers along the top of the water. "It's fine. Really. We keep Sadie away from Keane, Fia doesn't die. It's that simple."

"You can't keep hotel hopping for the rest of your lives."

I sink deeper, only my head above water. "I know. I know. But until I see something else, something that lets me know we're past the danger zone . . ."

"Did you tell Sadie?"

"No. How am I supposed to tell her the reason we're still running like crazy is because if she goes to Keane, my sister will murder her and then jump off a building? Besides, she seems like she's doing well. I like her. She's a sweet girl."

"I think you should tell Rafael. He can help figure something out. He has no idea why you three aren't stopping somewhere, and he's genuinely worried about you."

"Can we trust him?"

Eden hesitates. "He hates James and Mr. Keane. Maybe more than you do, even. He's not going to do anything that will help them. You can't fake that kind of hate."

"I'll think about it. I don't know how much longer we can keep this up. I feel like I'm fraying apart at the edges. You know?"

"I know. I can hear it in your voice. Things will work out. I promise."

"Liar," I say, but I'm smiling.

"Love you."

"Love you, too." I hang up, let the phone drop over the side onto the stiff hotel mat. I replay the vision over and over, trying to find some detail, some hint that the time period it happened in is over. But the windows are too high, so I can't see any trees for season clues. I don't know what Fia's hair looks like to compare it, or James's. And Sadie looks the same as she did in my other visions.

Sadie doesn't deserve this. The whole point of keeping her out of the school was to make sure she had a safe, happy life. Every night in a different cheap hotel with Cole and me, every day underwritten by a current of stress and strain . . . this is not protecting her. This is ruining her.

At least, unlike Adam and me, she's not pretending to be dead. She's emailed her mom a few times, let her know she's alive and safe. I can hear the TV in the room, still blaring the cooking channel that Sadie finds everywhere we go. Of the three of us, she's the most okay with this situation, when she should be the least okay with it.

I slip down until only my nose is above the water.

Something has to change.

When I stumble out of the bathroom, shivering from sitting numbly for so long in the freezing bath, I can hear the soft sounds of Sadie breathing in the farthest bed. I wonder what she's seeing, what futures are playing out in front of her eyes. She's whimpering in her sleep. She does most nights. She sees things while she's dreaming—not as bad as when she touches someone, but bad enough that she stays awake as long as she can every night.

I walk until my calves bump against my bed, then lean forward to pull the blanket back.

My fingers touch skin. Cole must have fallen asleep, waiting for me to come out of the bathroom. I mean to pull my hand away but his stomach is soft, so soft, and warm enough that I flatten my palm instinctively against him. I can feel the waistband of his pants and the bottom of his shirt where it's ridden up to expose this bare strip.

Things have been changing the last few days, stretching and shifting, until I could swear there was a sort of current between us. Now, touching him, it's completely alive with electricity. And I know with sudden and perfect clarity that I want him.

I have never *wanted* so much with my fingers. I want to crawl them up his stomach, under his shirt, feel the muscled contours covered by skin that has no right to feel this way. Tender. Delicate. The idea of any part of Cole being delicate is so incongruous that it snaps him into a whole new light, a whole new way of seeing him.

The image in my head I've built of his face, hard angles and narrowed eyes, evaporates, replaced with . . . warmth and softness. I have no idea how to picture him anymore.

I don't realize my hand is still on his abdomen until his own comes down on top of it. "Annie," he says, voice thick with sleep, but it isn't a question. It's a statement.

I start to move my hand, embarrassed, but he grabs hold of my wrist, pulls it around his waist toward his back so that I have to climb on the bed or fall over it. "Annie," he says, and now it sounds like a question, and I can feel the same question burning through me. He brings my hand up, brushes his lips across my wrist, and I crawl against him, my shoulder beneath his arm, my head in the curve of his neck and shoulder.

My own lips find his skin there, and I realize I want to feel him. I want to taste him, I want to know this strange new Cole, this warm and soft in the night Cole. I put my palm against his cheek and he leans his face into it, then shifts his body, arm wrapped around my waist pulling me on top of him.

"Annie," he says, and this time it is a sigh that I seal with my lips against his. They're full, almost hot against my own, and I can taste my name on them, taste how he sees me in the way his mouth moves across mine, lips gentle and searching. Then he rolls, flipping me onto my back beneath him, his chest and stomach and hips hovering just over mine, his lips so close to mine I can feel the air between us, charged like the moment before a thunderstorm breaks. I cannot stand it, cannot stand this tension, so I arch my back and wrap my hands behind his neck, pulling him down to me.

He makes no sense, this boy with velvet-soft skin, lips that promise nothing and everything and make me forget that anything exists except this space we're in. A space that is getting smaller, tightening around us, wrapping us together in a puzzle of arms and legs that I don't ever want to solve.

"Annie," he says, and it's a question again, aching and hopeful, and I don't know the answer, I only know how I feel and how I want to keep feeling, so I pull him closer, and then—

Sadie screams.

Cole lets out a heavy breath, his weight on me no longer tense as he relaxes his muscles and drops, then rolls to the side.

"What?" I say, flustered, my heart racing. "What's wrong, Sadie?"

She takes a gasping breath. "I saw it. I saw it. I've never seen myself older, and now I know why. I'm going to die. I'm already dead." She dissolves into shuddering sobs and I sit on the edge of the bed, helpless, not wanting to go to her and accidentally touch her, make it worse.

"How?" I whisper.

"It doesn't matter. None of it matters. You can't help. I'm dead."

I sink into myself, feeling useless. Then I sit up straighter.

I'm not useless. I can take care of her. I will. "I *can* help. I know exactly how you feel. I've seen myself dead, too. Three years ago, I was supposed to be shot in the head. And I'm here with you."

"Your sister changed it?"

"Yes." I try to sound as hopeful and sure as I can. "She did. So we can change this."

Sadie lies back down, the bed creaking beneath her. "Your sister is the one who makes it happen. Nothing is going to change. I'm going back to sleep."

"Sadie, I—"

"Leave me alone."

Cole's hand comes down on my shoulder, and I follow him into the bathroom.

"We're not fixing it, then," he says.

"We might be—she didn't tell us what she saw, maybe—"

"Annie."

I put my hands over my face, then sit on the edge of the bath. "Okay. Okay. Obviously this isn't working. We need to try something else. I think we need to tell Rafael, bring him in. He has resources. He could send Sadie out of the country, somewhere remote."

"I don't trust him not to take advantage of Sadie's ability."

"Neither do I. Not after the way he let Sarah fall apart. But he's not going to let Keane get Sadie. He'll get her somewhere safe."

I wait for Cole to argue, but he sits on the floor next to my legs, then leans his head against them. It feels so open, so vulnerable it's an actual pain in my chest. I rest my hand on his head, feel his hair, coarse with a hint of curl, between my fingers.

"If you think it's best," he says.

I try to laugh, but I can't quite manage. "I have no idea what's best. But I think it's our only option."

Rafael wastes no time. The next afternoon we meet him at a small airport.

"Annie, bella, I've missed you." He kisses my cheeks and I try to smile but I can't.

"Get her somewhere safe. Far, far away."

"You're sure, though, about what you saw—Fia was there, and so was Mr. Keane?"

"I'm sure. When I watch my sister die I pay attention."

"Forgive me. Of course. I'll take care of it; no one will be able to reach Sadie. There's another plane waiting for you two. We have a safe house in North Dakota. Adam and Eden are there now, and I know they'd love to see you."

"Thanks. For everything. Sadie?" I reach out and she moves forward. I pull her into a careful hug. "It'll be okay. You're going to be fine."

"Thank you for caring enough to try. Good-bye, Annie."

I've never heard such a final sounding good-bye.

* * *

"So are you guys doing it yet?" Eden asks, handing me the popcorn bowl. In the last seven days since we got here, I have eaten more popcorn than I thought was humanly possible. But at least Eden understands how to make a good pot of tea.

"Shut up," I hiss. "Where is he? He might hear you!"

"Relax. He's upstairs. But, man alive, that guy wants you. And the tension between you two is, like, wow. I have to keep taking cold showers so I don't jump Adam to try and work some of it out of my system. You are really bad to be around for a Feeler, you know that?"

I giggle. "Good thing Adam is at the lab so often. I don't think he could handle you. But really, I don't know what Cole and I are. We had a . . . moment. But things were so crazy and stressful, and then Sadie had to go, and we came here." I've thought about our kiss. So many times. Constantly. But I don't know how to bring it up.

"Rooming with me is cramping your style."

I smack her shoulder. "No, rooming with you is awesome. But it's like, how do you even start dating in a situation like this? Is it possible?"

Her phone chimes with a text. "Rafael. Sadie is in Europe, on her way to the Swiss Alps. Dang, girl, why couldn't you have seen Fia murdering me? Sadie gets the Swiss Alps, we get North Dakota. This is really not fair."

"It's not funny." The image of Fia doing that to Sadie, and then . . . I shudder.

"I'm sorry. You're right. You know what you need? An actual date. You and Cole should go out to dinner."

"I don't want to leave you and Adam out."

"Adam's not back from the lab until late tonight, anyway, and I make a mean microwave meal."

I bite the inside of my cheek. "But Cole and I have pretty much been living together for months now. What do I say? 'Hey, remember that time a week ago we totally made out in a hotel? That was nice. I'd like to do it again. Let's go to dinner.'"

Cole's voice comes from right behind me. "Um, okay."

My cheeks burst into flames. I pick up the popcorn bowl and dump it on Eden. She shrieks, laughing hysterically. "The look on your face . . . oh, that was worth it, I'm sorry, I'm the worst friend ever, but I will never regret this."

I turn to Cole, who must be behind the couch. "I was—you weren't—she was just—"

Laughter pulls the edge of his voice, stretching it into a shape that turns my embarrassment into something giddy. "Actually, I was coming in here to say the exact same thing to you. What a coincidence."

"Oh, really."

He walks around the couch. "Yes. Shall we?"

I hold out my hand and he takes it in his.

And—

Holy crap.

Holy crap, holy crap, holy crap.

"What's wrong?" he asks.

It's *his* hand.

"I think she's having a vision," Eden says.

"I—I—no. I'm not." I shake my head and he lets go of my hand but . . . I'd know that hand anywhere. It's his.

It was his all along. All this time, he's taken my elbow or my arm or my shoulder, but I've never actually held his hand.

"You okay?" Eden asks. "You look like you're going to pass out."

"I, uh, I'll go get my jacket." I rush past them, banging into the doorframe, then stumble around the tiny bedroom until I hit a low bed. I collapse onto it, unsure whether to laugh or cry, the things I'm feeling too much.

Cole.

I shove my fist into my mouth, laughing. I'm going to fall in love with Cole.

Actually, I'm pretty sure I already have. I pull the pillow over my face and laugh into it. And I didn't fall in love with him because his hand was right. I wanted him before I knew it was him. That makes it feel even truer somehow.

And then my stomach turns with a sick twist, because I can see. And it's not what I want to see, I don't want to, but I can't stop it.

A beautiful man sits on a leather couch, leaning back with his legs crossed. His skin reminds me of the way coconut oil smells. His suit shines beneath the overhead lights, perfectly contoured to his every line. His hair is black and curly.

Next to him is Sadie, brown hair back in a ponytail. Baggy clothes—long sleeves pulled down over her hands, long pants, wide-set eyes darting around the room like they can't settle on any one focal point. She's curled into the corner of the couch, legs tucked protectively in front of her chest.

A heavy door opens and two people enter the room. One, carefully handsome James, something tight and frightened around his eyes but not showing in his broad smile.

The other is the owner of the voice that still haunts my nightmares. Blandly handsome, not quite as tall as James but almost, the family resemblance in the jaw and the set of the shoulders. Phillip Keane.

And then a third person comes in (please no not again, not this) and my heart twists to see Fia, my Fia, but she doesn't move with her dancer's grace. James and the coconut oil man both look at her at the same time, each trying to convey something with sharp, expectant expressions.

She giggles, a high, nervous sound, and the line of her eyes shifts them into a shape I don't recognize.

She reaches behind herself

and pulls out a knife

and throws it, the knife sinking deep into Sadie's chest.

The beautiful man shouts, his hands fluttering over the knife and the blood as he tries desperately to help Sadie, who looks sad and resigned.

No one is watching Fia, who drifts to the balcony and jumps.

Eden's voice shatters the light, plunging me back into darkness. "Annie? Annie, what's wrong? What's going on?"

I gasp as though coming up for air from the depths of an icy lake. "Cole. I need Cole."

She runs into the hall and I'm alone with the things I saw. It changed, but not in the way it was supposed to. Why did it change that way? What was different?

Oh, no.

Oh *no.*

"What?" Cole asks, out of breath. I can hear Eden panting behind him.

"What does Rafael look like?"

I know before Cole speaks what he will say. "Curly black hair. Olive skin."

"He betrayed us," I whisper. "He's taking Sadie. He's taking her to Keane."

FIA

Nine Hours Before

I SIT ON A BRANCH, HIDDEN BY THE NIGHT AND THE clinging leaves, my back against the tree trunk. The lake stretches out in front of me, a black slick, but if I only look up, all I see are branches and leaves and sky. No lake, no park, no city. No buildings.

No people.

Rafael's plan is simple, and very similar to James's. He has guaranteed me Phillip Keane at an exact time in an exact place. He does not care what method I use, as long as Phillip Keane never leaves the meeting. And as long as Phillip Keane ceases to be, Annie is safe.

In Rafael's plan.

In James's plan, as long as Sadie ceases to be, Annie is safe.

If Phillip Keane were supposed to die, if that were right, if I knew what right was, then I would have let that woman kill him. I wouldn't have to decide to do it myself. It would already be done.

If Sadie were supposed to die, if that were right, if I knew what right was, then I wouldn't have wanted to protect her, wouldn't have wanted to save her. When I looked at her I saw myself.

But if she is me, I can't save her anyway. No one can.

I can't decide to kill either of them, so I take them out as variables. I make them not-people. They are not-people. They are elements of the wrong stretching out before me, and my goal is to choose the least-wrong possible.

This is easy. Rafael is wrong that makes me want to throw up. I should never have called him. I do what James asks. Rafael is implicated in the fake attempt on Phillip Keane's life. Annie remains secret and safe. Rafael is no longer playing any game at all.

Ever.

I get two taps for the price of one. A Sadie tap and a Rafael tap. I tap tap tap tap tap tap experimentally on the side of my leg, and I want to sink into the rough bark of the tree, be folded into its green heart, cease to exist think feel be.

I'll make myself a not-person, too. If Sadie is a not-person, and I am a not-person, then it doesn't matter what we do to each other, what I do to her. What I do after.

I pull out the stolen phone. The picture on the sleeping screen is a smiling, chubby baby. It is amazing to me that such a thing can exist. How does it survive? How does it live in this world?

I dial another phone number I know by heart.

"Hello?" my sister says, and I let out a breath of gratitude and relief, because she is alive, no matter how many times I forced myself to make her dead in my thoughts and feelings and heart. She's still alive.

"Heya, Annahell," I say.

"Fia. Oh, Fia. I have to tell you—"

"Are you safe?"

"I am."

She's not. She's never safe. It's my fault, always my fault. But I'll make this safe permanent if it's the last thing I do. "Stay safe, okay?"

"Fia, listen to me. Don't do it. Please don't do it."

I tap tap tap tap the back of my head against the tree trunk. She knows. She always knows. She's already seen what I'll do. She only sees the terrible things about me.

There are only terrible things to see when it comes to me.

"There's no right choice," I say.

"There is a right choice. Walk away. Right now. Just walk away."

I sigh, the breeze carrying away my breath my life my future my self. "I love him. Why would I love him if I wasn't supposed to?"

"Oh, baby sister. We all want things we shouldn't have. Even you. Just because you love him doesn't mean you should. Love is a choice, like anything else."

She's wrong. I had no other choice from the moment I met James. "I don't know what to do."

"Listen to me. If you do whatever course you're set on right now, you . . . Just don't do it. Promise me you won't do it. Don't hurt Sadie."

I was right, then, to pick James's plan. I already did in Annie's future. "I'm broken. I don't know anything anymore. I can't feel it like I used to."

She sounds desperate, sounds like before when she thought we could get out of this mess together. "Let me feel it for you, then. Let me make this choice."

We breathe together for a while. I wish I could see her. No. I don't. Not with what she's already seen me do. I hope I never have to see her again. "I'll figure it out," I say, taking my eyes off the sky and looking toward the city, toward where James has probably been waiting for me for hours now, frantic. "I always do."

"Not this time. Please, Fia."

"Don't worry about me. It's my job to take care of you, remember? Stay out of this. Stay safe. That's all I want."

"I'm coming—"

"No." I sit up straight. "*No.* You stay far away. Stay far away where you're safe. I'll be fine. I'm always fine."

"Fia—"

"I love you, Annie. Go live. I won't call again."

I hang up. I won't. I will never call her again.

I wander back to the hotel. I don't know what time it is until James opens the door and yells it at me as though it has any meaning whatsoever. And then he takes me and holds me, but I don't lose myself in his arms.

There is nothing left to lose.

I am already gone.

ANNIE

Fourteen Hours Before

~

I SIT ON THE FLOOR AGAINST THE BED, NUMB WITH horror and shock. "Do you have Rafael's number?"

"Yes," Cole says.

I hold out my hand. "Call him. Let me talk to him."

"I don't think—"

"*Call him!*"

His voice is soft to balance my scream. "Okay."

"What can I do?" Eden asks, her hand on my shoulder.

"We need to know where Fia is. Is there anyone you can call, anyone with Keane you trust?"

"I know where Keane headquarters is," she says. "I'll get tickets on the next flight to New York and text Adam what's up."

I nod.

"Here." Cole puts a phone in my hand and I listen as it rings.

"Who is this?" Rafael answers, his voice lacking all the musical play it had when talking to me. I was such an idiot to ignore that his voice changed when talking to women.

"You lied."

"Annie? Bella, how are you?"

"You didn't keep Sadie out of it."

"Ah." He sighs. "Has something ever been so important to you that you'd do anything? Anything at all?"

"Yes," I hiss. "My *sister*. My sister is that important to me."

"I'm sorry, Annie. I really am. But we all have the same goal, and now I have a way to make it happen. I finally have a meeting with Phillip Keane, and he won't survive. You remember Casey?"

"Don't change the subject."

"She's dead. Keane had her pumped full of heroin until her heart stopped and then dumped her body in an alley in Harlem."

"You're a liar," I whisper.

"I am not lying about this. I wouldn't do that to Casey's memory. I'm sorry for using you, but I can help look out for Fia. Tell me what happens in your vision now."

"You die."

"Don't lie to me."

"You *die*." I drop the phone.

"What did he say?" Eden asks.

I shudder, thinking of Casey. I don't have Fia's talent for spotting lies, but what Rafael said felt true. Too much. This is all too much. I think I'm going to be sick. "I need to go to New York myself."

"You can't go," Cole says. "If they knew you were alive . . ."

"I don't care. We get Fia out. Whether she wants to leave or not. And we save Sadie. Tell Adam to pack up his research and leave. We can't let Rafael have it."

"He's not answering his phone," Eden says. "I'll leave a message and a text to call us ASAP. There's a flight leaving in two hours. We can make it, but there's a layover in Minneapolis. We'll hit New York in the morning."

"Let's go," Cole says.

We've been in the Minneapolis airport for an hour when my phone rings. Breathless, I answer.

"Heya, Annahell."

Her voice is like a physical blow, punching through all the hollow spaces inside me where she used to live.

"Fia. Oh, Fia. I have to tell you—"

"Are you safe?"

"I am."

"Stay safe, okay?"

"Fia, listen to me. Don't do it. Please don't do it."

I hear a ghost of a tap-tap-tap-tap on the other end of the line and it buries me in a wave of grief. I'm mourning her like she's already dead, but she's not, she won't be.

"There's no right choice," she says.

"There is a right choice. Walk away. Right now. Just walk away."

The whisper of her sigh against the phone makes me ache to hold her close, the way I used to when we were little.

"I love him," she says. "Why would I love him if I wasn't supposed to?"

"Oh, baby sister. We all want things we shouldn't have. Even you. Just because you love him doesn't mean you should. Love is a choice, like anything else."

"I don't know what to do."

"Listen to me. If you do whatever course you're set on right now, you . . . Just don't do it. Promise me you won't do it. Don't hurt Sadie."

"I'm broken. I don't know anything anymore. I can't feel it like I used to."

"Let me feel it for you, then. Let me make this choice."

She's quiet, and I strain against the phone, listening to her breathe, counting on each breath, needing to hear them.

"I'll figure it out," she says, and now she sounds distracted and far away. "I always do."

"Not this time. Please, Fia."

"Don't worry about me. It's my job to take care of you,

remember? Stay out of this. Stay safe. That's all I want."

"I'm coming—"

"No. *No.* You stay far away. Stay far away where you're safe. I'll be fine. I'm always fine."

"Fia—"

"I love you, Annie. Go live. I won't call again."

The line goes dead.

"No no no no no," I moan, letting my head drop. "No."

And then—oh please not another one I can't see this again—light.

I watch my sister die.

In the vision, the beautiful traitor sits on a leather couch, leaning back with his legs crossed.

Next to him is Sadie. Dark circles under her eyes making her look older than sixteen.

The only door opens and two people enter the room. This is hell, watching this happen over and over again, not being able to change it. There is James. There is Phillip Keane.

And then there's Fia, my Fia, who looks from Sadie to Phillip Keane and back again, slides along the wall next to the door, shoves her fist into her mouth as though suppressing a scream. James and Rafael both look at her at the same time, expectant and demanding.

She giggles, a high, nervous sound, and she looks less than human, somehow.

There's a loud noise from the hall, a shout, and then something slams against the wall. The door flies open again and a man, ferocity in his blunt, young face, bursts into the room, fighting with another man in a suit. They fall to the ground, a tangle of vicious pounding limbs.

And then

And then

And then

I walk into the room, sightless eyes wide with terror, a gun that looks too heavy clutched in my wildly shaking hands.

Phillip Keane raises an eyebrow as though seeing someone he thought was dead happens every day. Fia's shoulders collapse and I can see the life draining from her even though nothing has happened yet.

"No," she says.

I hold the gun out, but I'm pointing at nothing, and everyone knows I won't shoot, can't shoot, can't even see what needs to be shot. Phillip Keane is to my right, James Keane is to my left, Fia is sliding along the wall to get behind me.

The two men still beat at each other on the floor and I think—I know—help will come too late. It's too late. I'm useless.

Fia puts a hand on my shoulder, reaches from behind me, takes the gun from my hand. "Good-bye, Annie," she says, and she doesn't sound sad. She sounds . . . gone.

Then she raises the gun and

She shoots Sadie in the head

Or

She shoots Phillip Keane in the head

It changes—shifts back and forth between the two realities so quickly I can't figure out which happens, which will happen, which did happen. It is all a blur of heads and bullets and dying.

But the ending is always the same.

She puts the still-smoking gun under her own chin and pulls the trigger again. Darkness returning brings no relief. My head is buried in Cole's chest, and he strokes my hair, telling me it will be okay.

It won't.

"We're there," I sob. "We try to stop it and it doesn't change anything."

"We still have to try," he says.

And he's right. This is the tragedy of knowing my fate: I have seen how it ends, and I will walk right into it, and nothing will change.

FIA

Six Minutes Before

ONCE UPON A TIME, I WAS A LITTLE GIRL WITH A MOM and a dad and a sister, and the only monsters in the world were imaginary.

Then I became one of the monsters.

Once upon a time I thought I had done enough to keep Annie safe. I thought that if she was gone, if we were separated, we would finally be free to make our own choices.

But I was wrong. She was still in danger. She was always in danger. We had it backward. *I'm* the problem. As long as I'm alive, Annie isn't safe. As long as I'm alive, no one who should be is.

One more. One more thing. I'll do one more terrible thing, one last terrible thing to keep her safe.

And I won't think beyond that.

ANNIE

Ten Minutes Before

~

I BLINK AWAY THE LIGHT, TREMBLING AND SHAKING.

"Again?" Cole asks, his voice soft. I've had the vision four more times on the way here. It doesn't change.

It never changes.

Cars honk behind us, the city louder than I could have imagined. We're outside the building where Keane's offices are on the top floor. I feel like we're on the edge of a cliff, and I know we'll fall, and I know exactly what the impact at the bottom will feel like.

I can't save Fia. I can't even protect Sadie.

"Are you ready for this?" Eden asks, her voice falsely bright with bravado. "Because I'm down for kicking some serious Keane butt."

"You're never there," I say. "In the room."

"Well, we're going to change that, aren't we. We're going to change all of it."

I wipe under my eyes and nod, but I don't feel it. Nothing is going to change. I push my sunglasses back over my face and hold out my hand. We've agreed it's best to avoid being recognized for as long as possible. I have to pretend to be sighted.

I'm expecting Eden's hand, but it's Cole's fingers that twine with mine. I let out a breath of exhausted laughter.

"What?" he asks.

It's his hand. There's no doubt. I don't know how there ever was any. "In case it changes, or we all die or something, I want you to know that I'm going to fall in love with you."

He's quiet, and I wonder how I can worry about something this silly right now, but I'm afraid he'll take his hand back. "Sorry. Was that weird?" I try to smile, but Cole's right. I can't smile when I don't mean it.

He squeezes my fingers and traces his thumb along mine. "Actually, it's a relief. Now I know you won't knee me for doing this."

He leans in and brushes his lips against mine. It's not as desperate as the kiss on the bed. It's a feather of a kiss, a promise of a kiss, and I hope with everything in me that it's a promise we'll be able to keep. I just don't see how there is a future in which that will be possible now.

"Well then," Eden says. "If no one's going to kiss me, let's get this show on the road."

We walk through a door into the odorless air of a lobby. Cole doesn't pause, walks confidently, and I do my best to match his pace.

"Excuse me, miss?"

I nearly freeze, but Cole pulls my hand, insistent and steady. I don't stop.

"Yes?" Eden asks, and her voice is farther behind us than it should be.

"I'm going to need to see your ID." The guy talking sounds apologetic.

"What for? I've never had to show it before."

"Sorry. I don't make the rules, I'm just the security guy."

"So, what, you're supposed to stop every black person that walks through here, because we couldn't possibly belong in a fancy building? Could you be any more racist?"

"No, that's not it at all! I only—"

"I want to speak to your supervisor."

Cole stops, and then there's a light ding. We step over the threshold of the elevator.

Eden isn't with us.

Just like I knew she wouldn't be.

The elevator slows and I take a deep breath—then there are lights, no, no, not again!

By the time Fia kills herself, I am leaning against Cole, barely standing.

"What are you doing here?" a voice hisses. I know this voice.

Cole speaks. "We're here with Mr. Marino. It's urgent."

"You can't lie to me! I know Annie."

Please, Mae, I think. *Fia's going to die.*

"Oh, no," she whispers. There's a buzz and a click. "Come on!"

Cole grabs my hand and runs forward. I'm dragged behind, trying my hardest to match his pace.

"Hey! What are you doing here?" I know this voice, too. Nathan. "You can't go back there!"

"Mae, what's going on?" another man asks.

"It's a setup! Rafael Marino is after Mr. Keane," Mae says.

"Is that true?"

"No!" Nathan shouts.

Cole lets go of my hand and I back up until I hit the wall.

"We have a situation!" the Keane security guy says, met by crackling static. There's the meaty sound of a fist connecting with a face, and he cries out.

Someone hits the wall next to me. I know by his cologne that it's not Cole. I jump on Nathan, throwing my arms around his neck and wrapping my legs around his torso.

"Go!" I scream.

I hear Cole run. I can feel a gun beneath my thigh, where

it hits Nathan's hip. I let go of his neck and grab the gun as he slams me into the wall and I drop to the ground. The vibrations of his feet pounding the floor follow Cole. Someone fires a shot. The security guy shouts, Mae screams, and I hear bodies slam into a wall. Then the sound of a door opening.

I stand, the gun heavy and cold in my hand. I know what it looks like. I've seen it so many times now. I know I will get into the room without being stopped.

I know my part.

I walk toward the end.

FIA

Two Minutes Before

PIXIE LOOKS UP AS JAMES AND I WALK BY.

"Fia, wait. Can I talk to you? Please?"

I don't think anything at her. I don't think anything at all.

Left foot, right foot, James's hand on my shoulder, guiding me. Left foot, right foot, so much can be accomplished without active thought. We pass through the doorway. I see Sandy blond with a gun, standing sentry in the hall with one of our security guards.

Ours.

Keane's. Ours. Mine. Doesn't matter.

Outside the room James stops, squeezes my shoulder but I don't feel it, not like I ought to, I don't feel anything. I'm a not-person. Not not not not. Tap tap tap tap.

Tap.

His father joins us. James opens the door and walks in, his posture perfect and his steps confident and his smile his very best, most assured lie. Rafael and the girl are waiting.

I follow, sliding along the wall, because I am a not-person and not-people take up no space in rooms.

I look at Phillip Keane, but he doesn't look at me, because he already knows I'm a not-person, he's known all along. He made me this way. I look at the girl on the couch, but can't keep looking at her, because if I keep looking at her, the girl on the couch will be a real person, and even not-person me can't kill a real person.

There is a strange sound that wants to escape from my mouth. Can't let that sound out. Teeth against knuckles to keep the sound in.

Something slams into the wall, and then the door bursts open, and two more people (not-people? Who can say anymore) tumble into the room, fighting. Cole and Sandy blond. I have fought both of them before. Cole should go after his knee. It's probably not fully healed yet. But who should I want to win? I cannot sort through anything to tell what will happen, what should happen, if I should make something happen. I have fallen into a black hole of wrong and there is no feeling here.

And then Annie follows them, a gun in her shaking hand.

"No," I say, and it makes me a person again but

no

no

no

Annie is a person. She's the only person, the only real person in the whole world, and now everything is over forever, no matter what, because she's here now and Phillip Keane is staring at her and he knows, he knows what I did, I'm a person again, I'm a dead person and it doesn't matter

nothing matters

nothing matters anymore, there is no safe, there is no way to fix this, I do what James wants and Annie is dead, I do what Rafael wants and James hates me forever, either way, either way I lose. I'll pick an ending and then I'll be done.

I put my hand on Annie's shoulder and reach for the gun she's pointing at nothing, because the gun is an ending. It's a fast ending.

Annie's shoulders droop, but then steel runs through them and she elbows me in the stomach. I jerk backward, shocked and hurt and—she hurt me?

"No," she says, her voice soft but made of the same steel that took over her shoulders, and I don't know this Annie. This is not the Annie from my dreams, the young and innocent Annie among the flames of my destruction.

"You don't get that future, Fia," she says.

She moves the gun from pointing at nothing to pointing

directly at Phillip Keane. He does not have time to look surprised before she pulls the trigger and with a deafening pop Annie creates an end.

James cries out. Phillip Keane is on the floor with a hole in his head.

I am still here. I didn't do any of this.

Annie did.

ANNIE

After

~

MY HAND HURTS, BOTH FROM THE WEIGHT OF THE gun and the force of the recoil. "Nobody move," I say, and my voice comes out steadier than I thought it would. "I know where everyone in this room is."

I've certainly seen it enough times. But not this part. This part is new. I made this part.

"Cole, did I kill Mr. Keane?"

"Yes." His voice is even and I hope he doesn't hate me now. But I don't regret what I did. Maybe I will, but not today, because I protected Sadie and I saved Fia. They needed me, so I did it. And Fia needs more saving.

I swing the gun to where I know Rafael is sitting on the couch. If I knew for certain that he was going to hurt me or Fia again, I'd shoot him. I wouldn't hesitate. But I don't have that guarantee, and I can't justify it. "You. Leave. If you ever come near me or my sister—or Sadie—again, you're a dead man."

"Annie," he says, "we're on the same side. Now that—"

"You set this up. You set us all up. We are not on the same side. Don't think I will ever forget that you were willing to destroy my sister. *Get out.*"

I hear the creak of leather as Rafael stands.

"This isn't over." James's voice surprises me. It's tortured, strained, full of more honest emotion that I've ever heard from him.

"Far from it," Rafael answers. I hear someone else stand and leave the room, and that's when I remember Cole was fighting with Nathan. I had completely forgotten to take Nathan into account. But I didn't need to. Cole was with me.

I reach my free hand back until I find Fia's. It feels small and cold, and I wrap it in mine, tug her gently forward until I can feel her body at my side.

"May I get up and see if my father still has a pulse, or will you shoot me, too?" James snarls.

I lower the gun, feel James walk in front of me.

"I'm sorry," I say, because I am. "It had to be done."

It did. I am as certain of that as I have ever been of anything. So many deaths—too many deaths—because of this man. He can't hurt us anymore.

"You're ruined now, too." Fia's voice is sad, so sad. "I couldn't save you."

I lean my head against her shoulder. "This was my choice, Fia. I made the right choice so you didn't have to make a wrong one. *I* saved *you.*"

"What now?" she whispers.

"I honestly have no idea." The only future I'd seen is gone now.

"You could have stopped this," James says, dazed and lost.

Fia leans closer to me.

"She couldn't have," I say. I changed everything. I took what fate had laid out for us, and I made a different choice.

"No one's going to kill me." Sadie's voice is relieved and puzzled, and very, very small. James clears his throat of a strangled sob. Fia drifts in his direction, then stops, tethered by my hand.

James sounds exhausted, but there is that edge of anger to his voice, the edge that has always been there. It sounds hardened, now, baked in a fire to a razor-sharp sheen. "I wasn't lying, Fia. We were almost there. I was so close." He stands, his voice getting distant. I imagine him looking out the window, back turned to us all. Fia lets out a strangled, lonely sound, and I squeeze her hand tighter.

James continues. "My father killed himself. He discovered his accounts were drained almost dry, that another company had bought controlling shares in all his endeavors, and that there was a whistle-blower whose information would have sent him to prison. I'm going to find his body in here in a few minutes, along with a note."

"We'll be leaving, then," I say, relieved. But it also makes me wonder—how had Fia never questioned James's comfort level with disposing of bodies? "Come on, Sadie."

"No, I don't think so." His change in tone freezes me in place. "You have powder residue on your fingers, you are on all our security footage, I have multiple witnesses putting you in the building. You leave. I never want to see you again. As far as I'm concerned from this time forward you really are dead. Sadie stays with Fia and me."

"You can't—"

"I *can*," he snaps. "Unless you want to shoot me, too, and figure out how to get out of this mess on your own. Be my guest, Annie. Blow my brains out."

I stutter, my mind skipping through ways around his demands, but . . . I have nothing. I have no leverage. I saved Fia for now, but I didn't save Sadie.

"No?" James asks, mocking me. "Then get out of my building before I call security."

"You have no money," Fia says, sad.

"What are you talking about?" He takes a breath, then sounds kinder. "Come here, Fia. It's okay. I'll let Annie go. My father—I—" His voice catches and I wonder if it's an act or if it's real. "I didn't want this. But it's done, and you're safe, and we can move on now. Everything he had is mine. We can finally move on."

"Everything you had is *mine*," she says. She moves closer to me, and I realize someone is standing on her other side. A low murmur lets me know that it's Mae.

"I don't understand," James says.

"All the accounts. All the money. I hid it."

I don't know whether he sounds angrier or sadder. "Why would you do that?"

I feel her shoulder move in a shrug next to me. "Just felt like I should. Been doing it for months."

"Fia." Her name is a growl coming from deep in his throat. "I know this isn't what you had planned. And I'm sorry I let you think we were going to destroy everything and then walk away. But I can't. We can't. I owe it to my mother to see to her legacy. People know girls like you, like Sadie, exist now. They're not safe. If we're here, if we're in control, then we are the most powerful and we can keep them safe. Together."

"I love you. But I can't—" Her voice changes; she's turned her head away, toward the window. "I can't stay. I can't live with what you wanted me to do." Another small shrug, like she's trying to shake something off her shoulders. "What I would have done."

Mae chimes in. "Annie gets the school, and oversight into everything you do with the girls in your networks."

"Absolutely not."

I hear Fia whispering beneath her breath, "A Keane is a Keane is a Keane, my Keane. I'm going to burn the school to the ground."

"You have no choice." Mae sounds matter-of-fact, like a

teacher explaining the rules on the first day of class. "If you don't do what Fia says, you'll have nothing left. She's listing account numbers in her head right now. She had access to everything, and you never checked up on her. I'm sorry, sir." The sarcasm positively drips from her voice. "She never thought about this around me. Otherwise I definitely would have reported it to you like a loyal employee."

"Secrets," Fia says, and I can hear the smile on her voice but it doesn't sound like a happy smile. "Even from you, James. Especially from you."

"Fine." His teeth strain the sounds of the words. "We'll talk about this at home. There's no reason to make a decision now. I have a dead father to take care of."

"I'm not going home," Fia says.

Fia is pulled away from me. "I'm sorry," James says. "I'm sorry for everything. I shouldn't have asked you to do this. I was scared, and desperate. I thought we could handle it together, like we've always done. This doesn't have to— this isn't the end. This is the beginning. You and me. I love you. I can't lose you. Not now."

"I love you, too. But that doesn't make it right. I can feel that now, I think." Fia takes my hand again, turns me around.

"Fia," James says, and for once he doesn't sound angry. He sounds lost.

Fia doesn't go to him.

"You can't burn it to the ground, Fia," Mae says, voice teasing.

"So stop thinking it. Annie and Cole will work out the details of the school with James after the funeral."

"Yeah. Come on, Sadie," Cole says. I feel safe with him here, shielded from James so that I can focus on Fia.

She walks forward and I walk with her. "Good-bye, Pixie," Fia says. "I'm sorry. I lied about everything."

"You can't lie to me." Tears play at the edges of Mae's words. "I always knew you liked me, you stupid brat. I'm coming with you. I have a suspicion I'm out of a job as a receptionist. My typing skills sucked anyway."

We walk out to the elevator, Mae talking down security, saying exactly what they need to hear to turn around and leave before finding Mr. Keane's body. Eden is waiting in the lobby, flirting madly with the guard. "Well," she says, huffing. "It's about time."

Together, we walk out. Five very not-dead girls, plus the love of my life. This future was never supposed to be any of ours. It wasn't one Sadie saw, or I saw. It was one Sarah couldn't begin to hope for, to the point where it drove her mad. It was a future not even Fia could make for herself.

This is *my* future. The future I made happen.

We are free.

The New York day is bitter cold and devoid of sunshine, but I'm warm.

FIA

After

~

"I NEED YOU." ANNIE SCOWLS IN FRUSTRATION AND disbelief. "I can't do this without you."

I smile, because she always has been the worst liar. "You can."

"But I don't want to." When I don't answer, she changes tactics. "What about Adam? He's going to be in Chicago near the school. We have to keep an eye on what he does, help him. And he's in love with you, Fia."

I zip up my bag, tap tap tap tap the zipper, try to think of anything I've forgotten.

I'd like to forget nearly everything.

Adam, sweet gray eyes long fingers Adam. "I hope he finds someone who can love him back."

"But where will you go?"

I close my eyes, breathe deeply, think of nothing. I need to be nothing. I need to be nothing for a very, very long time until I can decide what something I want to be. "James bought me a sailboat."

"He *what*? I thought you two weren't speaking." She stands, alarmed. She has a right to be. Most minutes it's all I can do to breathe without him.

"It's okay. He doesn't know he bought it for me." I can't figure out whether the idea of seeing James or never seeing him again hurts more. I don't want to talk to him until I can decide. We walked the path together, but he almost took me so far down it I would have fallen off the edge. Not even he could have caught me then.

Annie laughs, and I wrap my arms around her, bury my face in her hair, soak her in enough to last me for as long as I need it to.

"I can't believe I'm saying this, but . . . I think James has the right idea. Granted, I don't trust him to actually do it well, but someone has to be here. Someone has to find these girls and help them before they get taken advantage of like we were. I think we're doing a good thing."

"You are," I say, smiling. Annie is staying. I am leaving.

It is right.

Funny, what a freeing thing right is. And how . . . flexible it is. There is all sorts of right available to me now. Before, when

I had to choose between Adam and James, I chose the hardest right path. It almost killed me. For now, I'm choosing the easiest right path.

It's time to go. "Tell your grouchy boyfriend I said good-bye."

Annie blushes deeply, touches her lips. "He's not my *boyfriend*."

"I'm rolling my eyes," I inform her. "A lot. And take care of Pixie for me."

"I will."

I smile. I know she will.

And me?

I have a date with the endless empty ocean. I am ready to leave.

I am choosing nothing, and, for once, *nothing* is exactly right.

acknowledgments

For this, my sixth novel, a list of people who helped me along the way:

Noah, always, for being the foundation of my entire life and making it a happy one.

Elena, Jonah, and Ezra, for filling that life with more joy than I thought possible.

Erica Sussman, for always seeing through what I actually wrote to what I meant to have written, and helping me get there. Also for timeline angsting with me.

Michelle Wolfson, for being so much more than a literary agent—a friend, a business partner, and an ever-willing substitute curser for those times when I want those four-letter words but just can't say them myself.

Natalie Whipple, for reading way too many drafts of this book and supporting me through all of them. Also for naming the book. Also for pretty much everything. Annie will always be yours.

Carrie Ryan, for reading not one but two books to be able to offer me a critique, and for making me realize (in the nicest, smartest way possible) that I needed to start completely over before it was too late to do so.

Stephanie Perkins, for our joint insanity that goes so far in keeping me sane. Meet you at the cottage?

Shannon Messenger, Daisy Whitney, and Jon Skovron, for various industry venting services—I value your friendships more than my suckily infrequent emails would indicate.

The phenomenal team at HarperTeen: Christina Colangelo, Tyler Infinger, Casey McIntyre, Michelle Taormina, Stephanie Stein, Jessica Berg, and everyone else I've had the privilege of working with. You make awesome books, and I feel so lucky to be a part of HarperTeen.

Mom and Dad, for creating a childhood in which I never doubted I could be a writer for a living. All the rest of my very large family, both natural and married-into, for the support and friendship.

All the friends who have been a part of my life, and the ones who will doubtlessly come in a future that I, fortunately, cannot see: thank you for liking me.

And finally, always, to my readers. The space in your heads you rent to me one book at a time is a very great privilege indeed. Thank you.

FALL INTO A WORLD OF ROMANCE,
DECEPTION, AND ENCHANTMENT WITH

Keep reading for a sneak peek!

One

Dear Mama,

I am most certainly not dead. Thank you for your tender concern. I will try to write more often so you don't have to worry so between letters. (Because a week's silence surely means I have fallen prey to a wasting illness or been murdered in these boring, gray streets.)

School is going well. I am excelling in all of my classes. (Apparently, some things never change, and girls are not challenged in Albion in the same way they weren't on Melei.) *My professors are all intelligent and kind.* (Kind of horrible.) *None stand out.* (I refuse to mention *him* by name, no matter how many obviously "subtle" questions you ask.) *The other students are also quite focused on their schooling, and none of us has much time for socializing. Boys and girls attend separate classes as well, so no, I have not met many interesting young men.* (I am neither courting nor being courted. Please stop hoping.)

Tell Aunt Li'ne thank you for the mittens. They are very much appreciated in this cold, damp climate I am so unused to. And please tell the sun hello and I miss her very much! I also miss you, of course. (I do. Very much.)

All my love,
Jessamin

Reading over the letter to my mother, I am so absorbed in my head with adding the true statements to my written words that I fail to pay attention to the street. I cannot decide which shocks me more—nearly being run over by the horse-drawn cart, or the fluid stream of cursing in my native tongue that is being directed at me.

I look up, cheeks burning, and meet a pair of black eyes that, combined with the familiarity of the language, hit me with a longing for Melei so deep and painful I can scarcely draw a breath.

The man pauses, obviously surprised to see how dark of skin and eyes I am in spite of my school uniform. And so I take the opportunity to insult his manhood, his lineage, and his horse in a single, well-crafted turn of phrase I haven't used since my friend Kelen taught it to me when I was fourteen.

He smiles.

I smile back.

Brushing his hand through the air in another gesture so achingly familiar it brings tears to my eyes, he clicks his tongue and the cart moves on, our near-collision forgotten.

He's made me crave heat. The sun's anemic rays pull more warmth from me than they offer. I hate Albion, the whole gray country. I hate Avebury, a city just as gray, teeming with people but coldly lifeless.

No. Homesickness does me no good. Wiping under my eyes, I straighten my shoulders and march toward the hotel. I only have a couple of hours before my shift to do my reading for tomorrow's classes, and I will not be anything less than the best. I cannot afford it.

I cut away from the main thoroughfare and find myself in a narrow alley. It's old, the lines not quite vertical as they lean ever so gradually overhead.

"What's wrong, chickie bird?"

I startle, my eyes whipped down from where they traced the line of the sky. A man with the thick build, intricate tattoos, and accompanying ripe scent of a dockworker stands directly in front of me.

"Nothing." I flash a tight, dismissive smile honed these last few months of learning to blend in. "Just passing through."

"Nah, don't do that." He steps to the side as I do, and his

mass blocks me from walking by. "Come have a drink with me, yeah? Make you feel all better."

"I have somewhere to be."

His smile broadens, blue eyes nearly lost in the tanned squint lines of his face. "You ain't from 'round here, are you? An island rat, that's what you are." He reaches out with a meaty hand to touch my hair, black as night and waterfall straight, where I have it pulled into a bun at the base of my neck.

"Excuse me." I back up but he follows, leaning in closer. "Let me by."

"I've heard stories about island rats. You can tell me if they're true."

I lift onto my toes to sprint away when a hand comes down on my shoulder.

"There you are, darling. So sorry I'm late."

I don't know this voice, a low tenor with the clipped, stylish vowels of the classes I only see when delivering orders to their expensive hotel rooms.

I stiffen under his fingers, which are light but steady on my shoulder. Now there are two of them to deal with. I slide my hand into my satchel, gripping the handle of the paring knife I borrowed from the kitchen and keep with me all the time. The gentleman's fingers tighten.

"Not necessary," he whispers.

I turn to look at him—a low, round hat is pulled over his forehead, obscuring his eyes. His lips are sly and twisted into a smile over teeth far finer than my dockworker friend's. This man is a porcelain doll compared to the brute blocking my path.

He's taller than me but lean, all angles in his suit that reeks of money.

Apparently, the dockworker has the same assessment. "This your girl? I don't think she is."

"I would never accuse you of thinking, my good man." The gentleman lifts his silver-topped cane, tapping it once in the middle of the dockworker's forehead. "I shouldn't worry it'll be a problem for you to give up the practice of thinking entirely."

The dockworker blinks once—twice—so slowly I notice his stubby blond eyelashes, and then he moves to the side like he has forgotten how to walk on land.

"Good day, then." The gentleman steers me forward with his fingertips, and I've barely time to process what happened before we're out of the alley and back onto the main street.

"Well." I clear my throat, embarrassed. I look down the walkway instead of at the gentleman, not wanting to see in his eyes whether he did that out of the goodness of his heart or if he expects something in return. This is Albion, after all. "Thank you for your help. Good-bye."

"I'd like to walk you home, if it isn't too much trouble. Especially if you plan on gracing any more questionable streets with your presence."

I straighten my shoulders, sliding the right one out from under his hand, and look him full in the face. His eyes are dark, his features fine, almost femininely delicate, save his strong jawline. "With all due respect, sir, I'm not about to trade one strange man for another, and I have no interest in showing you where I live."

His smile broadens. "Then I insist you let me buy you supper, and we will part as friends with no knowledge of the other's residence."

I open my mouth to inform him I've no time for supper, but before I can, he takes off his hat and I find myself entranced by the impossible gold of his hair. I have never seen such hair in my life. It's like the sunshine of my childhood is concentrated there.

A door opens beside us, and his hand once again presses against my back. My feet trip forward of their own accord—*traitor feet, what's happening?*—and suddenly we're sitting in a warmly lit booth in a restaurant that smells of garlic and spice. My stomach and heart react at the same time: one with famished hunger and the other with renewed longing for home.

"I thought this would do nicely," he says, and his smile reminds me of the expression my mother's cat, Tubbins, would get when he'd done something particularly clever. "Why did you travel from Melei to attend school?"

"I never said I was a student. And how do you know where I'm from?"

"The beguiling way your mouth forms *S* and *O* gives away your island home."

I raise an eyebrow at his attempt to be clever. "It wasn't my dark skin and black hair?"

He laughs. "Well, those were rather large clues as well. As for the school, see—" He reaches across the table and takes my right hand in his. I try to pull it back, but his long fingers are insistent. "Look at your callus." He points to the raised bump on the top knuckle of my middle finger. "And see how it is stained black? If you were a secretary, no doubt they'd have you on one of those horrible new typewriters. You don't have the pinched look of someone who keeps ledgers, either. And, much like your skin, your school uniform is a bit of a giveaway."

I stifle a snort of laughter, not wanting to give him that point. Then, realizing he still has my hand in his, I pull it back and take a sip of tea. When did the tea get here? Have I been so distracted by his hair? I am not that shallow, surely. But I use the tea to buy myself a moment to look at him. "And what am I studying?"

He taps his chin thoughtfully. "In your final year of preparatory, yes? So you'd have to be in your focus. You have the soulful eyes of a writer and the heavy bag of a reader. Literature, certainly."

"History."

He narrows his eyes. "But that is not your first choice."

"Alas, apparently the feminine mind is not suited to the mathematical arts, all my test scores to the contrary. Now you, sir. Or is it 'lord'?"

"You may address me as anything you wish."

"Well then. You have all the grace and manners of nobility, not to mention clothes that cost more than our server's yearly wages. Your quick smile indicates an arrogance born and bred into you through generations of never having to answer to anyone, so I'm guessing lord, or perhaps earl, but lord suits your savior complex better. In your spare time, because being wealthy and privileged is a full-time occupation, you like mingling with those too far beneath you for notice. Chambermaids, waitresses," I glance meaningfully at where our serving girl is leaning against the counter gazing moons at him, "and even the occasional student. Unfortunately, sometimes you miscalculate your appeal and try to use your charms on girls who grew up on an island spotted with bastard children who were fathered by visiting Albens. I am therefore immune to being overwhelmed by your exceptional ancestry. You will, however, be able to console yourself with your vast lands and holdings and never again have to consider the student who paid for her own tea and then begged leave."

I dig out my purse and drop a few coins on the table, expecting him to sneer or curse, but instead I look up to find his first genuinely delighted smile. It makes him look younger and I realize he's probably not much older than me. Eighteen, perhaps.

"Oh, please stay and eat, won't you?" he asks. "I haven't had someone be so honest with me in ages, and I cannot tell you how refreshing it is."

Something in the open happiness of his face, the almost childlike hope there, whisks away my resolve to be cold.

"Very well." I sit back and consider my strange companion. "Though you haven't told me whether or not I'm right, my lord."

"I've no doubt you're right with startling frequency, and while I'd very much like to be yours, I am not a lord. Sandwiches to start?"

The meal is the best I've had since I left Melei. Halfway through, I'm struck with sudden fear for the cost of such a meal, but in one of those odd, sliding moments where I seem to be entranced by the light playing on his hair, the plates are gone and the bill is paid.

"Thank you," I stutter, unsure what else to say. I am out of sorts; I know we've spoken of many things, but I cannot grasp the particulars of any of it.

"Thank *you,* my dear Jessamin. Are you quite sure I can't walk you back to the dormitories?"

I stop midway to standing. "I told you my name?"

His sly smile is back, all innocence gone. "I plucked it from the air around your lips. And for the privilege of knowing it, I'll tell you that mine is Finn."

"Well then, Finn, I wish you the best of luck in your future endeavors, whatever they may be. I do not live in the dormitories, nor do I care to tell you any other details." I scamper from the restaurant. He follows, slower, and I turn to see him over my shoulder, watching me. When I round a corner toward the hotel, I check again to see if he is following, unsure if the thought makes me feel safer or scared.

A large black bird caws over my head, nearly startling me out of my boots. Frowning at it, I unlock the servants' entrance to the Grande Sylvie. Checking over my shoulder one last time, I notice a movement and jump backward.

I shake my head at my nerves. Only my shadow cast by the dim gas lamp.

But for the oddest moment it looked as though I had two.

DON'T MISS A SINGLE PAGE OF THE *NEW YORK TIMES* BESTSELLING PARANORMALCY TRILOGY!

www.epicreads.com